Dirty Little Secret

by

Sophia Ryan

Dirty Little Secret

COPYRIGHT © 2015 by Sophia Ryan

Contact Information: info@thewildrosepress.com

Cover Art by *Diana Carlile*

The Wild Rose Press, Inc.
PO Box 708
Adams Basin, NY 14410-0708

Visit us at www.thewilderroses.com

Publishing History
First Scarlet Rose Edition, 2015
Print ISBN 978-1-62830-772-6
Digital ISBN 978-1-62830-773-3
Published in the United States of America

His hooded eyes held tight on mine.

"This is the line, Angel," he said, his throat moving hard to swallow whatever was making his voice rough. "Once we cross it, there's no stopping. Be sure."

I was so ready for him. Had been for two years, since the first time I saw him, strolling like a badass across campus. I met his blazing gaze unashamedly, not wanting to hide the desire pulsing through me.

"I'm standing in front of you in nothing but my panties with my hand on your dick. Does it look like I want to stop?"

He didn't grin or laugh like I thought he would. His hand slid into my hair and cupped the back of my neck, his thumb gently brushing my cheek. "I need to hear you say it. Tell me what you want."

"Can't you tell?"

"Say it. I don't want there to be any misunderstanding."

I was embarrassed to tell him how much I wanted him, but I knew I had to or he wouldn't give me what I needed. I had to show him, tell him, make him understand.

I slid my hands back up the hard muscles of his stomach, his chest, his wide shoulders, my mouth following my touches with kisses and licks. Through it all, he stood tall, tense, almost as if he were trying not to feel what I was doing to him, trying not to give in until I said the magic words.

I looked into his eyes, my hands on his head, my fingers curled in his thick hair. "I want you, Nick Spencer," I said, not in a hesitant whisper, but in a low, bold tone that could not be mistaken. I leaned up on my toes and kissed his mouth, slow and deep, my tongue wakening his to the pleasure we would have.

PRAISE FOR AUTHOR

Sophia Ryan

SHE LIKES IT IRISH

"*She Likes It Irish* is a hot sexy ride. The characters are rich and well developed, the dramatic tension is high and the pacing is just right. I liked it a lot!"

~*Alberta, MR Review*

"*She Likes It Irish* is my new favorite read. I absolutely adored this book. The plot and story development will have you turning the pages just to see what happens next!"

~*Sarah Horwath, Fresh Review*

"*She Likes It Irish* has everything from quirky banter, sexy flirtation, sweet romance, devastating betrayal and heartache, and erotic, pulse pounding sex. I loved this book and did I mention yet, it is so hot?!?! Sophia Ryan should be my new best friend."

~*Sky Turner, Amazon*

Dedication

To the insightful reader who said about this book:
"This story shows that teens are passionate,
they feel, they love and have real emotions.
It's refreshing to read a new adult story that's
realistic." You get it. Thank you!

Chapter One

The second I settled into the buttery leather seat of Tyler Carrington's sleek sports car, I toed off the five-inch platforms to stretch and wiggle my toes, trying to bring the blood flow back to them that the too-cute-to-pass-up shoes had strangled throughout the dance. My feet sighed in relief. Or maybe that was me, glad this nightmare of a date was finally coming to an end.

Tyler closed my door and limped around to the driver's side of the car, the cast on his left leg making long work of the short trip. He opened the door, but before he could climb in, his friend Darius called out to him from across the parking lot.

"Yo, Ty. You and Angela going to the river?" he said, his voice heavy with innuendo.

"You know it," came my boyfriend's snickering response.

Ha! Not if I have anything to say about it.

"See you there, dude!" Darius yelled back and opened his car door for Mileah, his girlfriend.

"No, he won't," yelled Mileah.

Tyler laughed and, with a wave of his hand, slowly maneuvered his six-foot-tall frame into the low-slung seat, and snapped the seatbelt.

"Hey, babe," he said, leering at me with glassy eyes. "Ready to go?"

The smell of booze on his breath nauseated me,

and I turned my head and fumbled with the seatbelt to avoid it.

"Past ready." Irritation prickled my voice. I could feel his eyes boring into me, but his only comment was to slam his door.

As I buckled in, a voice inside me screamed, *Get out of the car*. Before I could agree and take action, the engine purred to life, the doors locked with a soft click, and Tyler pulled out of the parking lot onto the road. I stared out the tinted windows at the dark world flashing by me, dread filling the space around me.

"I had fun tonight, even though I couldn't dance because of this stupid cast," he said, referring to the leg he had broken at a basketball camp the week before school started two weeks ago. "How about you?" he asked when I didn't immediately respond.

He had started drinking an hour into the dance. Until then, it had been fun.

"Yeah, sure," I answered, and hugged my middle tighter to still the sudden nausea swirling there.

"Something bugging you?" he asked, irritation hardening his voice.

"Just tired." I probably should have told him the truth, but that would have started a fight, which would have prolonged the night, and I just wanted to go home. "I can't wait to get home."

His scoff at my response scratched against my skin to the thin layer of agitated nerves.

"Damn, Angela. You're a senior in high school, not a senior citizen. Try acting like it for a change. Have some fun."

He turned left instead of the right that would take me home, and confirmed what kind of fun he meant.

The blood in my veins boiled with anger, and thorns twisted like snakes inside my head. We were headed for the town's premier make-out spot.

"My parents gave me a one a.m. curfew," I said, "and it's almost that now. We don't have time to go to the river."

"Relax. They know you're with me, so they won't be worried."

Unfortunately, he was right. My parents adored him. Tyler's dad and mine were partners in the top law firm in our state, while our mothers were childhood friends who had been planning our wedding since we were toddlers.

But they didn't know him like I did.

The light of the full moon didn't quite reach us where Tyler parked his car under the ancient cottonwoods that flanked the river. The windows slid down, allowing the car to fill with the sound of water lapping the shore and the smell of lush, flowering trees. He cut off the engine but left the radio on.

Turning toward me, he rested his hand along my shoulders and massaged my neck. My body clenched in response.

"Tyler, I want to go home."

"I'm not ready to go home," he said, his voice harder than before. Tyler's fingers dug into my neck as he pulled me close for a kiss. He smashed his lips against my mouth, and his hand dragged roughly over my breasts, squeezing them. "God, I need you. It's been so long."

"Stop!" I pushed against his chest until he backed off.

He pounded the steering wheel with his fists.

"Dammit, Angela! You're my girlfriend," he gritted. "I shouldn't have to beg for sex."

"And I shouldn't have to fight you off when I've said no," I sliced back.

"You always fucking say no."

"I say no when you've been drinking, which is almost all the time these days."

"If I drink, it's to deal with your constant bitchiness. I'm fucking tired of it." His features were set in a tight snarl. "I'm not taking 'no' anymore." His tone had become sharp in a way that had my heart hiding in my stomach, and my body grew cold as if the heat had fled in fear.

Get out of the car, cried that little voice again. This time I heeded the advice. I unlocked the door but before I could open it, Tyler grabbed me by the waist and hauled me across the seat, my hip hitting the steering wheel, and my breasts smashing into his chest with a force that almost crushed my breastbone.

His arm lay like a steel band around my waist, holding me captive, while his free hand clawed up my dress in the back. Cementing my legs together, I twisted in his grasp and pounded on his head, his torso, wherever I could.

"I'm not having sex with you!" I seethed at him and at how defenseless I felt.

In the struggle, his elbow or hand collided with my face, and pain exploded in my cheek. The blow sent my head rocking backward and knocked me back into my seat. Nausea churned in my stomach, and I fought to tamp it down and ignore the throbbing in my face. I sat frozen in shock, trying to breathe, trying to calm the spinning, ringing pain in my head so I could understand what had really happened. *Surely he hadn't really hit me?* The buzzing in my ears quieted enough so that I heard a noise from Tyler's direction, and I realized he was speaking.

"Angie…Baby, I'm sorry. Are you—"

In that same stunned moment, I also realized he was no longer holding me. I pushed open the door and jumped out. Tyler grabbed my dress, halting my escape. I pulled hard to get away, so hard I heard the material rip. With a final hard jerk, I pulled free and ran. Despite the blow I'd just received, I wasn't really afraid of Tyler. I just had this overwhelming need to be away from him.

My heart pounded out extra spurts of energy into my sprinting legs as they led me deep into the dark maze of trees, bushes, and underbrush. Branches and thorns pulled at my dress and my skin like claws. Surrounded by the darkness and vegetation, feeling like it had swallowed me whole, I stopped and dropped to the cold, damp ground. My lungs heaved for breath, and colored bubbles popped around my head, but I held still, keeping my eyes and ears open for signs that Tyler was near.

I didn't hear the car door open, but I heard Tyler's shouts and uneven shuffle across the ground as he headed in my direction. In a matter of minutes, I heard his shouts of contrition change to fury when I wouldn't respond to his summons. Only when I heard the door slam shut, the engine fire to life, and the car drive away did I crawl out of my hiding place.

As I stood in the moonlight, the reality of my situation hit me. My phone sat in my purse in Tyler's car, which meant I would be walking the five or so miles home. In the dark. Alone. And barefoot because my shoes were also in his car.

"Smart move, Angela," I murmured with a groan as I wiped the cold sweat that dotted my forehead.

My feet sore from the rocks and sticks and other crunchy things I'd stepped on as I ran, I walked the few feet to the edge of the shore and stood ankle deep in the cool water. Scratches stung my arms and legs, and pain thundered in my head and my feet. My updo had come partially undone in the struggle. Dozens of tendrils flowed down from the braided knot that now hung askew on my head. The delicate above-the-knee champagne silk and lace dress that I'd special ordered was ripped in several places, from Tyler's clutches and the branches and thorny bushes, and one of the straps hung broken over my breast.

I felt hot tears on my cheek, and I swiped them away. I wasn't crying because of the pain; I was crying because I was pissed. The bastard had completely ruined another night. This was my last date with him. I would not go back with him, despite our parents' dream that we be a couple. I was done.

"Damn you, Tyler!" I screamed at the top of my lungs into the night.

My hands curled into fists, and I screamed again, a roar that expressed my anger and frustration at all he'd put me through, not just tonight, but for years. All the times as a child when he'd made me eat dirt, or tripped me, or grabbed my hand and made me hit myself, or ripped the arms and heads off my dolls. And laughed at my distress. That day he untied my bikini top at the club pool and took it off before I could grab it, and I had to climb out topless in front of everyone. The disastrous sexual fumbles. The guilt he used to convince me I should put up with his bullshit.

I picked up a handful of rocks and slammed them one at a time into the water, imagining it was Tyler's face.

"You're an arrogant, self-centered, mean son-of-a-bitch." Splash, right on his nose.

"Your dick's small and you're too drunk to get it up." Kerplunk, kerplunk, kerplunk, in the eye, the cheek, the forehead.

"I hate your guts, you disgusting bastard." A big one in the mouth.

In full fury, I bent down and grabbed more rocks. Bigger rocks. Raised one over my head and hurled it into the water, yelling, "I deserve better, you fucking asswipe!"

"I didn't know a mouth that pretty could talk so dirty." The smooth voice sliced through the thick night air from behind me, and cold fear replaced the hot blood in my veins.

For the first time that night, I doubted the intelligence of my decision to flee Tyler's car. I tightened my grip on my rocks/weapons and spun toward the voice.

"Who's there?" I demanded, putting a sharp edge on my voice.

The light from the full moon dusted the figure coming toward me. As he drew nearer, his face became more familiar. The planes and angles appeared softer than in bright daylight, but I knew that face, that body. My heart raced and my throat constricted, making breathing nearly impossible. I felt my chest rising high and fast. And I dropped my weapons.

7

He stopped three feet from me, his mouth settling into a wicked little grin. "Your worst nightmare."

Oh, no. Just the opposite. He was my dream. Nick Spencer.

I had devoted a forest of journal pages and rivers of ink to Nick Spencer since he had showed up in school our sophomore year. Practically every other journal entry vowed that if the opportunity to have sex with him ever materialized, nothing would stop me from taking it—not my family's uptight sense of class-based right and wrong, my snobbish friends, my fear, or any boyfriend I might have at the time.

A strange sensation gripped my body every time I saw or even thought about him, the same sensation that overtook me as he stood here now, close enough to kiss. Through the silky material of my ruined dress, my nipples puckered tightly as if being sucked by a loving mouth. I fought an aching need to press my thighs tightly against each other to relieve the tingling that throbbed between them.

I was in a dark, secluded place, completely alone with a guy I didn't know, had never been introduced to, had never even said hello to. Yet the fear I felt earlier had transformed into bubbling exhilaration. It took all my strength not to scream with excitement and jump up and down and clap my hands in pleasure at this happy turn of events. I hoped the semi-darkness hid whatever telling expressions might be playing out across my face and on my body. I wanted him, yes, but it wouldn't be wise to let him know it. Yet.

Forcing breath into my lungs also pulled his scent into my body. He smelled fresh, like the air after a rainstorm, a perfect counterpoint to the last-days-of-summer scents of the river. The intoxicating aroma—and his raging sexiness—fogged my brain and obliterated my ability to remember what proper behavior demanded in situations like these. I had to break the spell before I did something stupid, like wrap my legs around his waist, kiss him on that sexy, grinning mouth, and beg him to fuck me at the water's edge like in some old black and white movie.

"Actually, my worst nightmare is showing up to school naked." I heard the slight shakiness in my voice as I spoke the words. Nerves. With a dash of fear and at least a gallon of excitement.

The hazy moonlight hid details, but I clearly saw his eyes look me up and down. Slowly. Like he saw past my ruined dress to my naked body. Even though I probably looked like a disaster had exploded all over me, I felt thrilled by the thorough once-over.

"What you call nightmare would be considered a dream-come-true for more than half the student body. Do you always spend your Friday nights at the river, alone, barefoot, in a torn dress, and cussing like a rapper?"

When he'd said, "in a torn dress," he'd wrapped the strap that hung at my breast around his finger and tugged, his hand so close to my nipple that a battalion of goose bumps immediately marched across my body, pushing my nipple even closer to him.

"Do you always spend your Friday nights spying on people?" I asked. I was debating whether to slap his hand away when he released the strap and chuckled. The soft, low sound tickled across my body like a feather.

"I was here first. Maybe you're spying on me?"

I knew he was teasing, but it still unnerved me. I was losing control of this conversation, and I had to get it back.

"What are you really doing here?" I asked, letting my inner bitch drive. "Hiding from the cops?"

The minute the words left my mouth, I wanted to retract them. Especially when that sexy grin of his vanished along with the teasing softness in his eyes, showing me that maybe I had gone too far. I raised my hand toward him, opened my mouth, trying to get out the apology he deserved, when he stepped toward me. I closed my mouth, retracted my hand, and ignored the urge to step back. What was he going to do? Hit me? Kiss me? Unable to move, I kept my eyes on his, my breath on hold in my lungs.

He stopped with only inches between our bodies. "Is that what you really think?"

"No." The word brushed past my dry lips.

"Give me your hand." He held his out between us.

My heart jumped into my throat. "Why?" I asked, the tiny word struggling to get out.

"You wanted to know what I'm doing here."

Chapter Two

Feeling every prick of the slivers of fear I thought had vanished, I hesitated to give him what we both wanted.

You don't know this guy, my mind warned.

But I'd really like to, my heart cooed, sending a warm rush of desire through my veins that pushed my hand into his.

Holding my hand, he led me through a concealed opening in the growth behind us. It opened to reveal a grassy spot large enough to accommodate a spread blanket and his motorcycle. Lush tree branches, flowering bushes, tangling vines, and other growth screened the view from all sides, even disguising the low, narrow mouth facing the river. The moon acted like a spotlight, shining on us through the lacy canopy overhead as if we were the stars of our own play.

"So you are hiding," I teased. I released his hand and sat down on the blanket, expecting he'd do the same. Instead he walked to the beast and climbed aboard.

"But not from the cops," he said with a grin, telling me that maybe he had seen my regret and accepted my silent apology. His hands ran along the smooth curve of the handlebars, and my mind worked overtime wondering how it might feel to have his big hands touching my curves in the same, slow way.

"Great place for it."

"I showed you mine. Now show me yours," he said.

Confusion and surprise brought my brows up toward my scalp and made him laugh.

"What are you doing out here, all alone, other than practicing your X-rated vocabulary?" he clarified. His eyes searched mine as he spoke, as if looking for his own answers.

Struck by the force of his gaze, I looked away. I didn't want to tell him the truth—that I'd run away from my prick of a boyfriend and hadn't yet gotten the energy up to walk the five miles home. But what could I say? How could I explain why I was here, alone, with a torn dress and no shoes, at this time of night? I wasn't that kind of girl. Yet, here I was.

To give myself time to think of a sufficient answer, I raised my arms and began removing the dozens of bobby pins holding my nest of hair. The only response that came to me was a lame one, but I went with it.

"It's complicated."

"What did your boyfriend do to make you run and hide from him?"

My stomach flipped, knowing he was analyzing my appearance and could probably answer that question himself or that he'd heard everything and was waiting for me to admit it.

"Is he the one who tore your dress?"

My hands left my hair and dropped into my lap. "I'd rather talk about something else. Something interesting."

"Like?" he asked.

"Like…you." A smile on my face, I leaned back on

my palms, stretching my bare legs out in front of me.

His eyes dropped to my legs, and the thrill rushing through me made me bold. The next time he looked at me, I stared into his eyes, a smile in mine, willing him to come to me. To entice him further, I patted the blanket beside me.

"Come sit by me."

As if unable to resist my summons, he dismounted and came over. Slowly. He looked down at me for what seemed like ages, almost as if he was fighting wanting to join me. But then he lowered himself to the blanket beside me.

"What do you want to know?" he asked.

I was about to tell him when he leaned toward me, lifted his hands to my hair and removed a few of the pins I'd missed.

His gentle touch in my hair, his closeness, his smile, his smell, his voice had me melting into the blanket like a chocolate kiss melting in the microwave. A purr started in my heart and headed toward my throat but I swallowed it.

He dropped the pins into my lap and stretched out on the blanket, propping himself up on his elbow, his head in his hand, and stared at me.

"How about I ask you ten questions—any questions I want." Desire had thickened the blood flowing in my veins, and I wondered whether he heard it in my rough voice. "You can either answer or pass. But you can only pass twice."

"Then I get to ask you ten questions?" he asked.

"Right." Seeing his long, hard body laid out before me made me want to play another game, but Ten Questions was certainly safer. "Okay, let's start with something easy, like…What's your favorite food?"

"Steak. Rare. You?"

"Is that your question for me? I mean, you don't have to ask the same one I do."

"That's my question. Are you passing?"

"No."

He grinned. "Then answer it."

"No need to get bossy." I smiled at him to show I was teasing. "You and I have something in common. My favorite is filet mignon. I like it medium rare with a merlot reduction and sprinkled with English stilton—slivers, not crumbles. My turn. When's your birthday?"

"May twentieth. Yours?"

My heart flipped. "Seriously? That's my birthday too." The doubting look that crossed his face made me want to cross my heart with my hand and recite the stick-a-needle-in-my-eye rhyme, but I wasn't ten, so I went with the much more grown up "No, really." He hadn't said a word but was all but calling me a liar with that look.

"What day was *our* birthday this year?"

"Is that your question?" I asked with a teasing grin.

"It's a clarification."

"It's a question. The answer is Monday. I flew back early from my birthday celebration in the Keys because I didn't want to miss any school, so close to the end of the year and all."

He shook his head, grinned. "Of course you did."

I got the feeling he was laughing at me, but I chose to let it go. "My turn. Do you have any tattoos?"

"No. You?"

"No."

"Yeah, tatts don't really go with the whole good-girl image," he said.

Good girl. I know that's how he and everyone I knew saw me. And that was okay. I had my reputation to uphold. But wouldn't Nick be surprised to know that this "good girl" wanted to rip his clothes off, kiss and lick all over his fucking hot body, then do all kinds of kinky, nasty things to him. Yep. I, Angela Nicole Abbott, aka Ice Princess, had a sexual fire raging inside me that would burn everything in its path if I didn't keep a strong hold on it. It was part of the reason I put up with Tyler. Even though the sex wasn't great, especially when he was drinking, he was an acceptable outlet for my urges. I didn't want to discuss my quirks with Nick, so I chose to respond to his question and let his taunt go.

"I'm not opposed to tattoos. I just don't want one just to get one. It would have to have great meaning to me. Why don't you have any?"

"I don't love anything enough to want it embedded under my skin forever."

He looked away from me when he responded, and a mask of sadness flashed across his face. It made me sad to hear there was nothing he loved that much. In a way, it was similar to my reason. Neither one of us had found something special enough to give it a forever spot in our lives or on our bodies.

"What's your number one vice?" he asked, moving on quickly as if he saw something in my eyes that said I wanted to explore his response.

I grinned. "How rude of you to assume I have any."

"How predictable of you to assume you don't."

Before I could demand that he explain his

comment, he added, "Bet I can guess it."

"If you say something lame like shoes or jewelry, I'll be really disappointed in you," I teased.

He shook his head, and his eyes tangled hot with mine. "Sex."

Heat flamed across my face and ran a timed maze through my body before impaling itself in my crotch. I think I blinked a couple of times. My mouth suddenly felt bone dry, while the wet spot between my legs became wetter and my pouty nipples rose to pebbles in the lacy cups of my bra. I swallowed thickly.

"Chocolate." The word barely made it out. He grinned at my lie. Chocolate was vice number two.

I didn't need to ask him his vice. I knew that like me, he craved the physical satisfaction that only pounding sex with another person—the right person— could bring. I could see it on his grinning face. See it in his well-built body that oozed sexuality. I could smell it on his tanned skin, like a heady elixir that was meant to drive women wild. I inhaled deeply to still the desire swirling inside me, but his scent only sparked it. To help restore my calm, I went on like his words hadn't found my most intimate places and buried themselves deep like a pulsing signal.

"Favorite food, birthday, our stance on tattoos..." Sex. "Wonder what else we have in common?"

His eyes stared into mine, then dropped to my mouth. He licked his lips, and his eyes rose to mine again. We had something else in common: a desire to make out with the person sitting next to us on the blanket.

"Is that your question?" The words slid thick and slow out of his mouth, and I wanted to lean in and catch them on my tongue like drops of honey. I swallowed and pulled away from his gaze and my erotic thoughts.

"Is it my turn?" I asked.

He shrugged. "Go for it."

I thought for a moment, trying to come up with a nonsexual question. "Do you carry a knife?"

His eyebrows rose. "Why? Do you need one?"

"No, I don't need one. I was just curious."

"Do I look like a guy who'd carry a knife?"

Dangerous. Mysterious. Bad boy. Sexy as sin. Check, check, check, double check.

I shrugged, not able to control the grin growing across my face. "It's my turn to ask a question, and my question was—"

"Yes."

I about choked on my tongue. He carried a knife. With that one answer, the darkness became deeper. Our spot became more secluded. He became more dangerous. My body tingled all over, from fear, from excitement, from the way he stared into my face when he admitted to carrying a knife. How his face seemed to go a shade harder.

"Why?" I asked, my voice low, almost a whisper.

"It's not your turn," he said.

I sat upright and scooted closer to him, put my hand on his arm. "Can I see it?" Yeah, strange guy I don't know. I'm not in enough danger, so why not ask him to take out a deadly weapon too? That way I'll really be in trouble.

After a moment, he sat up and moved to his knees, reached his hand into the front pocket of his jeans, and pulled out a shiny silver object about four inches long. He held it in his hand, ran his thumb along it, and a thin, double-edged blade shot out the front of the small, coffin-shaped handle.

My stomach clenched. *Shit!* This wasn't just a knife. It was a switchblade. A switchblade that was now about eight inches long. Why did I invite this into our bubble?

"Can I hold it?"

He slid his thumb along it again and the blade retracted. He moved to sit right beside me, his shoulder against mine, his thigh against mine, no breathing room between us, and he took my hand in his, setting the knife in my palm. The weight and chill of the weapon sent an icy finger down my spine. I looked at Nick, found his eyes sparkling with humor as he watched my curiosity play out. I took a breath.

"Show me how to open it."

Our heads bent together, and I felt his breath on my cheek. It smelled like cinnamon gum. He helped me hold the knife correctly and showed me what I'd asked.

"It's a double-action OTF model, which means the blade automatically extends and retracts out the front when you slide this button."

"OTF," I whispered, and at the simple flick of my finger, the blade again sliced out.

Moonlight danced on the steely point and razor thin edges as I turned it. It was a work of art as well as a lethal weapon. And of course it was sharp. But stupidly I just had to test it. I pressed the pad of one finger to the tip and watched a drop of blood bloom on my fingertip.

He took my hand, brought it to his mouth, put my finger into his mouth, and let his tongue lave the tiny puncture. I felt the soft bite of his teeth, the small licks of his tongue, on my lips, on my nipples, on my clit, and it made me shiver.

"Have you used it?" I managed to whisper.

"You mean, have I stabbed anybody?"

I nodded, holding onto his dark gaze for dear life.

"Pass." He released my hand.

Oh shit. He had stabbed someone with that knife. He was the kind of guy who carried and used a switchblade. *Oh shit, oh shit, oh shit!* pounded out on the beats of my racing heart. Thick silence poured around us. We didn't speak, but our eyes maintained tight contact. I had the overwhelming urge to grab his head and lock lips with him, slide my tongue into his mouth like the blade had slid out of the knife handle, pull his breath into my lungs, taste my blood on his tongue.

He lifted the knife from my hand, retracted the blade, and set the safety. Then he rose to his knees, and shoved it back into his pocket.

The air seemed to change once the knife was out of sight and Nick had shifted away from me. He leaned back on his hands, legs out in front of him crossed at the ankles of his booted feet. It was as if we had spiraled away somewhere to another plane, but were now back in the present, alone in this dark, romantic spot, and everything was in stark focus.

The water lapping the shore. The clicks and rustles of various night creatures surrounding us. The purr of a car engine. The crunch of tires on the ground. The flash of headlights. Oh shit, a door opening.

"I think it's my turn," Nick said.

My hand flew to his thigh, squeezing it hard. "Shh!" I whispered.

Several feet away, shuffling footsteps crunched on

19

branches. Someone was coming toward us. And I had a bad feeling I knew who it was.

"Annn-ge-laaa! Where are you?" Tyler yelled.

Nick started to stand, but I scrambled up and climbed onto his lap, straddling him, my hands gripping the tight stretch of T-shirt at his wide chest. His arms went around me. Our eyes locked. I shook my head. Tyler would try to take me away from this place, from Nick. I didn't want that, and I didn't want the drama that would unfold when I said so.

"Angela! Get in the car. You know I didn't mean to hit you. It was an accident. I'm sorry, okay?"

"He hit you?" Nick's whispered tone screamed anger. The moonlight showed his narrowed eyes, his full mouth in a tight line, his tense body.

I didn't answer, just put my arms around him and tucked into his chest. Right now, where his body met mine was the safest spot on Earth.

"Son of a bitch." Nick's low curse rumbled through my body.

He moved to disentangle himself from my arms and get up, but I tackled him to the ground, hard, and lay on top of him, holding him down with my body, one hand over his mouth.

"No, Nick," I pleaded in a hush. "Please. Please, just stay with me."

Rustling noises sounded at the entrance to our paradise, and I held my breath.

"Babe, I had a coffee, so I'm sober now. C'mon. I gotta get you home. Your parents are going to be pissed. It's one-thirty."

Tyler wasn't a patient person, so it wasn't long before he became irritated at the effort of having to

20

search for me.

"Dammit, Angie! Fucking walk home, then." His angry eruption filled the night.

I heard his steps shuffle away from us and his door slam shut. The car spun out in the dirt, then peeled out when it hit asphalt, heading the opposite direction from where Nick and I lay together.

As the crisis passed, the here-and-now drifted back into focus. I inhaled a gulp of silent, sweet air, felt the anxiety leave my body on the exhale. It was then that I noticed the sexy clean scent of Nick in my nostrils. His hard body beneath mine. The comforting weight of his arms around me.

I raised my head from his chest, removed my hand from his mouth, and our eyes met. "Thank you." I whispered, though there was no reason to.

He hooked his leg over mine and rolled us so that he was on top of me. "Where did he hit you?" He whispered too.

"My cheek."

He lowered his head and gently brushed his lips across my cheek, along my jaw, and near my ear. Tingles of pleasure danced up and down my skin.

"Better?"

"It was the other side," I said, breathless.

He smiled and gave the other side of my face the same sweet attention.

"How about now?"

"He also got my mouth."

Nick moved closer, and I could taste the cinnamon on his breath as I breathed in.

He touched his lips to mine, just touched, but that tiny touch sparked a need so strong in me I knew this one simple kiss wouldn't be enough. I opened my mouth to him, hoping he'd be able to translate the little mewling moan that escaped my throat as "more."

Lucky me. He did.

His lips moved over mine, brushing back and forth, as if he were trying to learn the shape of my mouth. I sucked his bottom lip into my mouth, and he came with it, as if he needed to be closer. His mouth opened wider then, and he pressed his mouth against mine, angling his head, trying to find the best fit. The tip of his tongue teased inside my lips before delving deeper to stroke my tongue. The kiss grew longer, deeper, hotter, until the air in my lungs evaporated and all my reason blurred. He was giving me the kiss I'd always dreamed he'd give me, and all I wanted was more.

There wasn't a part of me that didn't want the touch of his fingers, his palms, his mouth, his body. Overfilled with need, I wanted to scream out, demand that he take me. All of me. Now. I had never been this swept away by one kiss, one touch, one guy.

"Touch me, Nick. Everywhere."

His eyebrow raised and he grinned. "You know my name."

I nodded, my eyes dancing over his. "And I'm—"

"Angela Abbott."

I grinned. He knew my name. "Yeah."

"Good to meet you." Then his mouth was on mine again. His hand rounded over my breast, pressing, kneading, tweaking my nipple. Wanting to touch me and not the material, his fingers moved to the row of tiny silk buttons down the front of my dress and tried to unbutton the first one, but unfortunately, they didn't lead anywhere; they were just for show.

"No." My mouth left his just long enough to deliver the command in an urgent, rough-with-need tone.

His hand jerked away from me, and he broke the kiss. Disappointment flared in his eyes, and he rose to his knees.

I rose to my knees too. "Zipper…" I explained, pointing over my shoulder. "There's a zipper." Nerves triggered a little giggle that pushed past my lips. "It's in the back." I turned to show him.

He grinned. "For a minute I thought I'd have to take the switchblade to those buttons."

The idea of him cutting my dress off with his knife to get to my body made me flame with desire. If I had other clothes to change into, I'd ask him to do it.

His hands slid up my back, feeling for the zipper. With one hand, I lifted my hair and pulled it over my shoulder so he could unzip me. My dress fell open, baring my back to the night air and to his touches, which started low and moved up to my neck. Chills washed over me, cooling my skin and hardening my nipples. I shivered when I felt his fingers unlatch the band of my strapless bra.

He slid the dress down to reveal my nearly nude front. His hand gripped my bra, and in half a second had it off. He stared at my breasts for a long few seconds. Was he worshiping them…or having a difficult time deciding where to start? Whichever it was, his long, slow, appreciative gaze made me feel desired, and knowing that he desired me that much made me feel powerful.

He rounded his hands over my shoulders and gently, lightly, ran them down the length of my arms, then up my stomach. Then his hands were there. At my breasts. On my breasts. Cupping. Caressing.

A jolt of unbelievable pleasure shot straight down through my core and wrestled a quick, high murmur from my mouth. I couldn't catch a breath, my chest rising and falling but getting nowhere, but it was okay because I wanted his touch more than I wanted to breathe.

My nipples puckered so hard they were pulling the skin around them taut and firm, rounding my breasts into a shape that fit his hands perfectly. He ran his palms over the hard points, then pinched them between his fingers, rolling them. Hungry, greedy need roiled at the core of me. My mouth opened in a soft sigh, and my hands gripped his hips and held tight so I could press my breasts deeper into his hands.

Part of me wanted to just close my eyes and luxuriate in his touch, but watching him touch me, watching the emotions playing out on his face, added to my pleasure, so I kept them open, watching him through half closed lids. The way his tongue darted out to wet his lips, the focused gaze following every movement of his hands on my breasts, the lacy breaths coming from his mouth—all told me he was as into it as I was.

His head lowered, and his perfect mouth rounded over one nipple and sucked. The delicious action pulled a ragged whimper from my throat and drew my hands up to cup the back of his head and hold him there. Then his mouth found the other nipple, his tongue lapping it like he was lapping hot fudge off me, and I couldn't help myself—my eyes fluttered closed in ecstasy.

I may or may not have cried out when his mouth

and hands left me, I'm not sure. All I know is that he did, and it left me deeply disappointed and painfully empty. I opened my eyes and saw him rising to his feet.

He extended his hands to me. "Stand up," he said, his voice rough.

I took his hands and stood, and my dress flowed down around my feet, leaving me standing in moonlight and sheer, lacy nude panties in front of him.

Releasing my hands, he reached over his back, grabbed his T-shirt, and one-handedly yanked it off and flung it aside. My eyes crawled over his wide chest, down his rockin' abs, and to the huge bulge in his jeans. Hot desire fluttered in my stomach at the thought of seeing his cock, touching it, taking it inside me, and it pushed me forward to take actions that would get me what I wanted.

Running my hands down his chest, slowly to feel every smooth inch, I paused to brush my thumbs over his nipples and felt a thrill of satisfaction when they hardened beneath my touch like mine had with him. I trailed down over his hard stomach, and the defined muscles contracted under my fingertips.

I could feel his eyes hot on me when I reached for his fly, and heard him suck in a breath as my fingers fumbled to pry the button from its hole. A sound, a low mmm, rumbled in his throat as I wrestled his zipper down over that erection. His hips flexed forward almost instinctually as I stroked the rigid outline of his rod through his boxers. I licked my lips then, holding my breath in my lungs and biting my lip, and slid my hand into the waistband of his boxers.

The smooth, hard knob of his cock waited right at the tips of my fingers. A needy groan jumped out of his mouth as I plunged in and grabbed him, but his hand flew to mine to stop me. My eyes flew to his, asking *WTF?*

His hooded eyes held tight on mine. "This is the line, Angel," he said, his throat moving hard to swallow whatever was making his voice rough. "Once we cross it, there's no stopping. Be sure."

I was so ready for him. Had been for two years, since the first time I saw him, strolling like a badass across campus. I met his blazing gaze unashamedly, not wanting to hide the desire pulsing through me.

"I'm standing in front of you in nothing but my panties with my hand around your dick. Does it look like I want to stop?"

He didn't grin or laugh like I thought he would. His hand slid into my hair and cupped the back of my neck, his thumb gently brushing my cheek. "I need to hear you say it. Tell me what you want."

"Can't you tell?"

"Say it. I don't want there to be any misunderstanding between us."

I was embarrassed to tell him how much I wanted him, but I knew I had to or he wouldn't give me what I needed. I had to show him, tell him, make him understand. I slid my hands back up the hard muscles of his stomach, his chest, his wide shoulders, my mouth following my touches with kisses and licks. Through it all, he stood tall, tense, almost as if he were trying not to feel what I was doing to him, trying not to give in until I said the magic words.

I looked into his eyes, my hands on his head, my fingers curled in his thick hair. "I want you, Nick Spencer," I said, not in a hesitant whisper, but in a low, bold tone that could not be mistaken. I leaned up on my toes and kissed his mouth, slow and deep, my tongue wakening his to the pleasure we would have.

I ended the kiss and eased back just enough to find his eyes again. "I want this," I said in the same bold tone as I dropped a hand to his hard cock and caressed it through his boxers. "I want you to fuck me with it. Is that clear enough for you?"

I was standing close enough to hear the groan that rumbled in his throat, close enough to see him swallow, close enough to feel his heart hammering against mine, leaving no doubt that he understood what I wanted and that he wanted it as much as I did. One of his arms snaked around my hips and yanked me tight against the front of his body, letting me feel the stab of the hard cock I'd asked for. His hand squeezed my ass while the other cupped the back of my head and pulled me closer. He crushed his mouth to mine.

He was a great kisser, his full lips soft but firm, taking and giving, the right amount of tongue, the right pressure, the right taste. I could kiss him all day and all night, but at the moment all I wanted was to get the rest of his clothes off.

Pushing out of his grip, I dropped to my knees, caught handfuls of his jeans at his hips and yanked them down his muscular legs. Then his boxers. His cock bounced out, as long and hard as his knife, and I reached for it eagerly. As I held his dick in my hands, enjoying the hard smoothness of it, I realized something horrifying.

"Oh, no," I moaned. I released him and sank back on my knees. And too late realized that probably wasn't the best thing to say while holding a guy's manhood.

"Too big?" he asked.

I grinned up at him. "I, uh, don't suppose you have a condom?"

"Do I look like a guy who carries around condoms?"

"Yeah."

Chuckling, he kicked out of his clothes and grabbed his jeans. He reached into one pocket and dropped a condom on my leg.

I picked it up. Looked at it. Then him. "Only one?" I teased.

"More than you brought," he teased back, without missing a beat.

I chuckled and ripped open the package. "Bring more next time." Then it hit me what I'd suggested. That we would do this again. My eyes flew to his. A hot little grin lifted his delicious mouth. Did I want to do this again? Did he? *Stop it, Angela! Don't overanalyze this gift. Just enjoy it.*

"Count on it," he agreed and fisted the base of his cock, steadying it as I unrolled the condom. His erection jutted long and strong, and I couldn't wait for it to turn my insides into liquid pleasure.

I pulled off my panties and lay back on the blanket, my arms splayed up by my head, waiting for him. He didn't immediately join me but just stood over me, watching me, his hand slowly stroking his dick.

"Are you having second thoughts?" I whispered.

"Are you?"

I'd waited forever to be with him like this. I wasn't stopping now, not when I was a heartbeat away from it. "No second thoughts. No doubts." I smiled and held out my hand to him. "In fact, the *only* way you're getting out of here alive and in one piece tonight is to get your freakin' hot ass down here and show me you know how to use that monster cock in your hand."

Even in the dark, I saw his eyes and grin flash with pride and pleasure. He seemed to stand taller, more magnificent, his chest lifted, his strong arms stronger and, if it was even possible, his cock bigger. In an easy, graceful move, he lowered himself down along beside me. I eagerly turned into his arms as he pulled me against his body, his cock stretched out along my stomach.

His arms around me, he kissed my mouth thoroughly as his hand moved to the vee of my legs. He stroked my pussy, not delving inside between my lips, but petting and massaging my mound, the soft touch driving me crazy with need to be touched deep.

Encouraging him, I wrapped one leg around his hip and pulled him close, felt his rock hard dick arching against me. A ragged growl left his throat when I fisted the throbbing pole and rode it up and down while rubbing the tight head of it against my stomach. His breath was labored, like mine, but his motions were sure and quick on my weeping pussy, like he'd done this before, like he knew just where to touch a woman to make it count.

The more I touched his cock, the more it seemed to swell, and the faster his hips rocked into me. He groaned in my mouth, left the kiss, and slid down, head at my breasts, so I could no longer touch him. I felt a sharp pain of disappointment until his tongue snaked out and licked the tip of one nipple into his mouth, making me rise up and press my breast closer to his mouth.

My nipples were painfully erect, straining up for him to take them. His licks, sucks, and bites brought some relief to one breast before he switched to the other, his lips nibbling the tip, his tongue flicking it, his mouth sucking it deep.

The pleasure of his mouth had me mewling in appreciation, but I wanted more. Needed more. As if reading my mind, he slid further down my body, kissing and licking and sucking all the way, marking my stomach, my inner thigh, and sending tingles all through my body.

I wanted his mouth between my legs, but it wasn't safe. Although I didn't have any STDs, I didn't know whether he did. Just last week I'd learned that guys who have HPV can give it to girls through oral sex, or vice versa. I knew I had to make a decision soon because he was headed that way. I ached to feel his tongue running all over my pussy, stroking my clit, fucking my tunnel, but I put my hands on his head and stopped him.

"Nick, we can't do…that," I said, my breath and heart racing.

He looked up at me from his spot between my thighs, his eyes bright in his shadowed face. "I'm clean, Angel." I was happy to hear his breath was as ragged as mine.

I hesitated. I really, really wanted it, but….

He licked up my inner thigh, inches from my mound, and sucked hard. Oh, that would leave a mark. Then he breathed on my hot sex, more of an ahh, followed by, "I want to make you come with my tongue."

His hungry growl and erotic words had all the moisture in my body pooling in that hot spot, almost making me come as I arched up. No one had ever said something like that to me. I wanted it, but I wanted to be safe more.

"Not this time."

He scrambled up my pulsing, writhing body, braced over me, his weight on his strong arms, looking down into my face. He kissed me, his lips eating my mouth as eagerly as he would have eaten my pussy. My legs went wide, and I reached between us, feeding his hard cockhead to my hungry cunt. He took control then, giving me what I needed, pushing deep inside my tight sheath, inch by inch. He was big and long and hard, but I was slick enough and horny enough to take him without much discomfort.

We both released a sharp "ahh" of pleasure at the union. I arched my pelvis against his, wanting to feel all of him inside me. His body went rigid.

"No," he gritted and pulled slightly out of me so that the head of his cock wasn't pressing against the mouth of my womb. He was straining, trembling, as if he was holding back a flood of emotion bearing down on him. "Fuck, Angel. Don't move."

Except for the rapid rise and fall of my chest, I held perfectly still. I looked at him. His mouth was tight, his jaw clenched, eyes squeezed closed, nostrils flared, the muscles in his arms tense and strained as he hovered over me like a plank.

Oh, God, no! It couldn't be all over with! Had he come already? When this had happened with Tyler, it had been almost a relief because he'd then use his hand to get me off, something his cock had rarely been able to do. Having it over with wouldn't be a relief with Nick. It would be a tragedy. Almost a killing offense.

We had no more condoms!

I knew the second he felt under control. His eyes opened and found mine. He lowered his head and kissed my mouth, his lips sliding over mine, his tongue teasing and tasting the inside of my mouth. The body that eased into mine was still hard but not tense. And he started moving, slowly, sawing his cock in and out of my slick tunnel in long, deep strokes that stoked my desire and left my mind blank of everything but what he was doing to me.

His hand moved to my breast and massaged it, and he moaned in my mouth at the feeling. Then his mouth left mine to suck the nipple he had erected. All the while, my hands flowed over the smooth skin on his back, down to his sexy, tight ass, pressing him deeper into me.

I lifted my head and licked and sucked and bit his shoulder, leaving my own mark on him and pulling a groan from his mouth that vibrated on my nipple. I felt him shiver so I did it again. And again. Anywhere I could reach. I wanted to taste him, bite him, lick all over his hard body—back, front, up, down, everywhere.

His mouth came back to mine and kissed me deep, increasing the speed of his thrusts.

The little sounds coming from my mouth showed my eagerness to have him all, to have him increase the pace. So did my actions. Lifting my legs, knees up, legs wrapped around him, I took him deeper inside me, my nails digging into his ass cheeks as he pounded into me.

"You like my cock inside you?" he rumbled against my open lips, his eyes on mine.

I cried out at his gravelly, sex-filled voice, a loud, embarrassing growl at the pleasure ripping through me.

"Yes. Oh, God, I fucking love it!" I continued to call out crazy unintelligible sounds as I came around his cock, squeezing it, encouraging him to come with me.

He pistoned into me, harder, deeper, faster, until he let go too, his sounds matching mine in intensity. He thrust against me once more and stopped, his cock twitching inside my spasming sheath.

Both of us gasping, flushed with exertion, satiated with pleasure, he sank into my body, his head tucked into my shoulder, his teeth grazing my neck. I held him tight to me, my entire body gripping him, inside and out, never wanting to let him go.

He raised his head and kissed my mouth gently, softly, lovingly. Then he rested it on my chest, trying to find his breath, trying to come back into himself. I'd told him I wanted him to fuck me, but he'd loved me, more than I'd ever felt. This wasn't love, but he made me feel loved.

I almost cried when he left me for a moment to dispose of the condom in a small plastic bag from his motorcycle, but then he lay back down beside me and held me. Trailing my hands lightly up and down his back and in his hair, I thought that if I could have kept him here in this spot forever, I would have.

As we lay together, the warmth of our breath drying our sex sheen, I didn't worry over the fact that I had shared the most intimate act two people can share with someone who was little more than a stranger—the things I knew about him could be counted on one hand. The extreme peace and utter satisfaction we had given each other filled me, pushing out all other thoughts like the consequences of my impulsive action.

Sometime later, I felt his hand at my breast again,

cupping it, caressing it, toying with my nipple that was standing at attention again under expert his touch. I'd had the biggest orgasm of my life with him, and I wanted him again. But we didn't have another condom.

I caught his hand. "Mmm, it feels amazing, but don't make me horny again."

"Why?"

"We don't have any more condoms."

He raised his face to mine. "There are other ways to make each other feel good."

"Yeah, but they're not as good."

"Says who?"

"In my experience, they're not as good."

"Then you've been with the wrong guys. Or girls."

My face flushed at his suggestion that I'd been with a girl, and I pinched his nipple. "I have not been with any girls."

His low chuckle rumbled through me. "I'll make it good for you," he said with confidence, as his fingers trailed down my chest, my stomach, my thigh. Then his hand was there, curving between my spread legs, and softly, gently, he caressed the plump wet flesh, stroking it. His fingers parted my pussy lips and teased inside, drawing some of the slickness up onto my clit and circled it slowly with the perfect amount of pressure. Wantonly, I lifted my leg to the side, opening my pussy more to him, giving him space to touch me everywhere.

"You like that?" He knew I did by my actions, my murmurs of pleasure, but I liked that he asked, his sex talk, his raspy voice adding another layer to ratchet up my pleasure.

I moaned my *yes*. I was so wet, and he used my juice to tug and rub my pussy lips, press my clit, tease the opening of my core, building up the pressure even more. Needing to touch him, I turned slightly into him, easily so as to not disturb the magic he worked, and my hand flew to his cock. He was hard already and slick and satiny, and I loved the feel and weight of him in my hands. I loved the smell of him. I let my mind focus on that hot, hungry area he was working between my legs and on the feelings going wild inside me at the touch of his fingers, at the feel of my hand wrapped around his dick.

When he pushed a finger inside me, I about came off the blanket, pressing my pussy against his hand, grabbing onto the feeling with all my body. He slid his finger in and out slowly, deliberately, all the while using his thumb to ride my clit.

My head was spinning, my breathing was shallow, my eyes closed, one hand on my breast pinching my nipple, the other hand on his cock. God, I was almost there already.

He thrust his hips against me, into my hand, as I stroked my hand up and down his cock, the wet head of his erection poking against my stomach.

"Imagine that my finger is my cock. And it's inside you. Filling you. Banging into you, making you come. Imagine me shooting my cum deep inside you." His slow, raspy voice urged me on.

I was imagining it, and it was so good.

"Nick!" I cried out as lights exploded behind my eyes. "Oh, Nick! Oh." Arching up into him, writhing against him, I came hard against his hand, marveling at the exquisite explosion rippling inside me. I released so fully that I felt drained, tingly, my toes numb, my body zinging.

His breathing was erratic as he pumped against my hand. I focused on him then, using my other hand to caress his balls, his swollen cockhead.

"Shoot your cum on me," I growled, trying out the nasty talk, and was rewarded seconds later. His eyes squeezed tight, and he tensed hard into me, then pumped harder and faster, his head arched back. Jets of white cum shot onto my stomach with every grunt and flex of his hips. I stroked him empty, then a little more just because I enjoyed it.

The smell of our sex wafted up between us in an intoxicating aroma that heightened the thrill of what we'd done. Seeing his cum shoot out of him and onto me was erotic and naughty and satisfying, and something I wanted to experience again. With him.

We stilled then, my hand gripping his sticky cock, his hand between my legs, his finger inside me, but not moving.

"You were right," I sighed. "It was good. Great, actually. But still not as good as having you inside me."

He cocked his eyebrow at me. "Are you always this difficult to please, princess?"

I laughed at his teasing tone. "Yes."

He laughed. "Good to know," he said, then kissed my smiling mouth.

When our breathing had settled and our hearts had stopped racing, he used his boxers to wipe his cum off us, and I again settled back into his warm, strong arms for more of his delicious wet kisses.

Later, amid silent and surprisingly shy longing looks, we helped each other dress. I put on my bra while he helped me into my dress and zipped it. He pulled on his jeans while I zipped and buttoned them—

carefully since he wasn't wearing boxers. I ran my hands over his chest one more time before handing him his shirt. Then standing in the moonlight, we held each other and shared long, sweet kisses and slow touches that were meant for no other reason than to extend our connection, to show our appreciation for what we'd shared with each other this night.

If I died at this moment, I could say that I had known true happiness—making love with Nick Spencer.

Chapter Three

The wind twisted the ends of my hair up and my heart rode high in my throat as we traveled the dark, quiet streets on his motorcycle. Even though we took the long way home, all too soon we arrived at my house.

Nick cut the engine a few houses away from mine and coasted to the entrance of the long, circular driveway before braking. I pulled off the helmet he'd insisted I wear and got off the bike, then climbed back on, facing him, my legs draped over his. He took the helmet and hung it on the handlebars. Our arms around each other, we kissed in the darkness.

"I hope you…I want you to know that I don't normally do this sort of thing," I murmured against his neck, unable to find the strength to leave his arms.

"What sort of thing—make out on a motorcycle?" He sucked at my bottom lip.

He was teasing, of course, but I shifted my face away from his searching lips and directed a serious look toward him. "What I mean is, I don't have sex with guys I don't know. I mean, I've only been with one guy and…Nick, I'm not a…" For some stupid reason, I couldn't speak. I lowered my head and tucked it against his chest.

What else did you call a girl who hooked up with a stranger than the words I was thinking? Easy. Tramp.

Whore. Slut. I'd labeled many girls throughout my years in high school with those terms, judged them as less than because of it, something to shun. Maybe I'd been wrong. I certainly didn't feel like a degenerate after being with Nick. I felt happy and good, more satisfied than I'd ever been. How could that be wrong? Not like I'd be making a habit of hooking up at the river. With him or with anyone.

"I know what you meant," he said, kissing my forehead, the top of my cheek, the corner of my eye, "and I know you're not."

"How do you know?" My question was labored—he had moved on to nibbling the delicate flesh of my earlobe, sending chills down my spine. "We don't know each other." I spoke slowly. It was hard work this talking thing when my brain was rushing signals of hot pleasure to all parts of my body and blocking out all instructions such as breathing and talking.

"Everything about you screams 'good girl.' That doesn't mean you don't like sex. It means you don't do it with just anybody." His voice was low and as seductive as the feel of his lips traveling down my neck and across the strip of skin left bare from where the strap of my dress used to sit.

My fingers curled in his hair to hold his head and mouth and tongue close to me. I didn't feel like a "good girl" with Nick, and he didn't feel like "just anybody." The thought ripped a purred moan from my mouth.

"I can't get enough of you." My words danced out in a voice full of rapture. God! I wanted him again.

His lips found mine, and he kissed me fully, sensuously. Then he pulled back, looked at me, and cupped my face in his hands. Moonlight flickered in his eyes and answered the whisper I was hearing all through my body.

"Come home with me, Angel," he said softly. "I want to spend the rest of the night making love to you."

"Making the rest of my fantasies come true?"

"Every one of 'em."

"I bet you could," I said huskily.

"I could. And at home, I have a whole box of condoms and the whole house to myself tonight," he replied and sweetened the offer with another convincing kiss.

His hands, which had been around my waist, dropped lower to rest on my thighs. They crept beneath my dress and slowly inched their way up my legs as he kissed me. My panties had been sacrificed to line the nest of some little critter that lived on the river bank, so Nick's wandering fingers had green-light access to the slick flesh between my legs. He brushed his thumbs against me, pleasuring me, and I leaned into his touch. I drew in a quick breath when one thumb gently circled my sensitive clit standing at attention just above the eager entry to my core.

"You're not making it easy to say no." The words sounded like they came from a person groggy from sleep or drink.

"Then say yes," he prompted and stopped moving his hands.

Every nerve in my body screamed "yes, yes, just don't stop!" but the small part of my brain that was not fogged over retained control of the unruly crowd. I leaned into him and hugged him.

"My parents would absolutely kill me if I stayed out all night."

"With me."

"With anybody." I was quick to answer because I knew what he was implying. "Like you said, I'm a 'good girl.' And 'good girls' don't stay out all night with a guy."

His hands retreated to a safer position atop his thighs, and he was quiet for a moment, his eyes searching mine as if he was looking for unspoken deception. "Is that all it is?" he asked. A lot of emotions rode the thin shoulders of those five words. Disbelief, accusation, sadness, regret only a few. The pulsing mix of it rocked me back to search his face for the truth.

"What do you mean?" I asked him.

"You know what I mean."

"I'm not sure I do."

"When we see each other at school, are you going to run into my arms and kiss me like you kissed me tonight, or are you going to turn away and act like you don't know me?"

The eyes that held mine sparked with emotion, but his low, even voice didn't. It was emotionally flat as if he'd already checked out because he thought he knew the answer.

Unfortunately, he wasn't wrong.

While I would want to choose his arms and kisses, I knew I would turn away. The separate worlds we lived in wouldn't allow anything else. But still I hesitated, not wanting to give my answer even while knowing it had to be done.

"That's what I thought," he said at my silence. His voice was now stone cold resolved.

"Nick." I wanted to say something more, something to ensure the last moments of our magical

41

night wouldn't simply disappear in hard feelings, something to erase the pained look in his eyes that I had put there. I went with the simple truth. "If you believe only one thing I tell you, believe this: Tonight, with you, was the best night of my life, and if I could go with you now to keep it going just a little longer, I would. But I can't."

He said nothing, and I couldn't think of anything else to say without hurting him more or lying to him, so instead I said the only thing left to say: the sad, painful words that would be the beginning of the end of this night. I leaned in and kissed him, just a brush of my lips against his. "Goodbye, Nick. Thanks."

I was ready to get off the bike and go in when he pulled me back into his arms. Sliding his arm around my waist, he clutched my body to his, one hand in my hair.

"*This* is a goodbye kiss." He brought his mouth to mine, and I hungrily took his kiss, his feel, his touch, and gave back in equal portions, causing the fire still burning inside me to flare. I wrapped my arms around his neck and held him tight, possessing him the way he possessed me. I leaned into his hardness and it amplified my hunger.

He buried his head in my neck, between my breasts, nipping and sucking my skin, leaving his mark on me for all to see. He dropped the softest, gentlest kisses we'd shared that night on my face, my chest, and my lips. And I let him, encouraged him by lifting my face to his, closing my eyes, parting my lips, giving his hands free access to my body.

Way too soon he eased back.

Taking a deep breath, he dipped his forehead to

touch with mine. I ran my tongue over my lips, tasting the cinnamon spice of his mouth that still clung to them. In silence we sat, glued to each other.

"Angel," he said finally, his voice so low it teased and trembled across my skin. "If you don't go in now, I'm going to make love to you again. Right here on my bike. Or there on your lawn by that freaky-ass gnome." His gaze met mine. "Or I'm going to start this bike and take you home to my bed." The look in his eyes said he was serious. "Your choice."

I knew I should leave his arms, knew I should go in, but I didn't want to. I didn't want to move away from him or from these fresh new feelings that, now awakened, demanded attention—the kind of attention only he could give. I was completely content, wrapped in our circle of warmth and passion. I knew that what we had shared could not last beyond the moment I left his arms, so I wanted to wring out every last bit of pleasure I could.

With a grin, he started the cycle and rocked it to move up the kickstand. Oh shit! I had to get off the bike now, or he'd take me home with him.

He had grabbed the helmet to give it to me to put on when the front door opened and my parents, both in their robes and slippers, marched out toward the end of the driveway where Nick and I had parked.

I scrambled off the bike, hoping the light where we'd parked wasn't good enough for them to have seen my legs wrapped around his hips, and me rocking my pussy against his pole.

When they got closer, the grim look on their faces told me they were not happy; their sharp words confirmed it.

"Angela Nicole Abbott, where the hell have you been?"

"We've been worried to death."

"Are you okay?"

"Why didn't you call?"

The questions came at me so rapid-fire fast I couldn't respond to any of them. Every time I tried, the other parent would fire a new question at me. I shot a "kill me now" glance at Nick, who wore a little grin on his face and seemed to be enjoying the scene.

"Mom, Dad. Please…one question at a time."

Dad, ever the aggressive, take-charge lawyer, spoke first. "Tyler called us, frantic, saying you had jumped out of the car and run off, and he hadn't been able to find you."

Mom, standing slightly behind Dad, arms crossed, chimed in. "What would possess you to do something like that, Angela? We raised you to have better sense."

I found an open spot and charged in. "Tyler was drunk and being a jerk. Did he mention that when he called to tattle on me?"

Silence fell over our odd little group, and I could see my parents struggling with how to process the information I had given them. I didn't know whether that meant they were having trouble believing that the prince they'd chosen for their princess was really a warty toad, or just having trouble believing my version of the night's events. They stared at me, then at Nick, then at each other.

"Let's take this discussion inside." Dad took one of my arms, Mom the other, and they ushered me toward the house. It bugged me that they said nothing to Nick, like thank you for bringing our daughter home, safe and happy. Or at the very least, who the hell are you?

"Just wait," I said and broke free and went back to Nick, despite their quick protests.

"Bet you wish you'd gone home with me," he whispered in a teasing voice.

I grinned, nodded, and rolled my eyes all at the same time.

"Ask me nice and you can still come."

We stared into each other's eyes. He reached out and ever so lightly stroked a thick strand of my hair between his finger and thumb, then caressed my face with the back of his knuckles. I put my hand on his and nuzzled my cheek against it, pressed a kiss into his palm. Our hands still smelled of our orgasms.

"Thanks for tonight," I whispered. "It was—"

"My pleasure," he whispered back before I could say "perfect."

"Angela, now!" Dad's voice behind us was firm.

I released Nick's hand, and he pulled on his helmet, shifted the bike into gear and, with a tip of his chin instead of the kiss I wanted, rode off into the night. I stood on the sidewalk and watched the darkness swallow him.

"Take me with you," I whispered. But it was too late. He was gone. Despite the warmth of the late-summer night, I shivered, feeling cold without his arms and kisses to warm me. My heart was as silent and deserted as the empty street.

After Nick disappeared around the corner, I sighed and turned toward the firing squad. Instead of stopping, I walked past them and into the house. It didn't take them long to start the questioning again.

"Oh my God, did he do that to your dress?" Mom

asked, her eyes wide with worry as her hands swept over my ripped dress.

"No." I swatted away her hands.

"Who was that boy and why were you with him on his motorcycle without a helmet?" Dad asked.

"His name is Nick Spencer. We go to school together. He gave me a ride home after Tyler stranded me at the river. Because of Nick, I wasn't walking the dark streets alone—and by the way, he insisted I wear his helmet. After all he did for me, I'd think you'd be a little more grateful to him instead of assuming he'd attacked me."

Mom's face went ghostly pale and she pulled her silk robe firmly over her chest. "Did you say Nick Spencer?"

At my nod, she touched her hand to her face and slumped against Dad as if she were feeling faint. Dad put his arm around her but continued his tirade as if it were a normal occurrence for her to faint against him.

"If you were in trouble, you should have called us to come pick you up instead of going off with some strange boy on a motorcycle. Those things are dangerous."

Strange boys or motorcycles? is what I wanted to say, but I went with something that wouldn't piss them off more than they already were.

"First of all, he's not some *strange boy*," I insisted firmly, "and second, my phone was in my purse in Tyler's car, so I couldn't call anyone."

"Spencer. Spencer. I don't recognize the name, and I certainly don't recall you ever mentioning him." Dad wore a pensive scowl—eyebrows furrowed, index finger pressing his lips—and I was sure he was mentally going over the country club membership roster to place the last name.

"Why are we even discussing Nick?" I said. "Why aren't you more concerned with how Tyler treated me tonight?"

"Tyler told us what happened and, frankly, I'm surprised by your lack of good judgment," Dad said.

My eyes flew wide open. "What load of crap did he shovel at you and Mom?"

"Load of crap? Is that the way you talk in front of your mother? Look how upset she is. If this is an example of this Nick's influence on you, I won't have it. I simply won't have it!"

Dad was right about one thing; Mom did look upset. She looked as if she were going to be sick.

"What did Tyler tell you?" I asked.

Though my question was directed to Mom, Dad answered for her. "He said you were upset because he and his buddies had a drink at the dance, you two argued, then you jumped out of the car and ran off. He said he searched everywhere for you but couldn't find you in the dark and with his leg in a cast, so he left and called us before going out again to find you. That was nearly two hours ago. What the hell have you been doing for two hours?"

"Having the best sex of my life."

Okay. No, I didn't say it. But I thought it. If I'd told them that, I'd have spent the rest of my senior year under house arrest.

"Tyler didn't have 'a' drink; he had several. He was being a jerk. I didn't want to be in the car with him. We argued, and I jumped out and ran away from him. After a while, he took off."

I don't think he had hit me intentionally, so I left that part out, and I didn't want to have a sex talk with my parents, so I also left out the part about Tyler being pissed because I wouldn't have sex with him.

"I was heading home when I ran into Nick. He gave me a ride so I wouldn't have to risk my life walking home alone."

"What was this Nick doing running around this late at night? Think about that while you're jumping to his defense."

"I can't believe you two are so in love with Tyler—or the idea of Tyler and me as a couple—that you're willing to ignore the truth. Tyler Carrington is a jerk, and I'm never going to date him again. Nick is a nice guy who helped me through a bad situation. End of story."

With that, I stormed up the stairs to my room and slammed the door on the sound of Dad yelling my name. I caught a glimpse of myself in the mirror hanging on the door. My hair looked like a tornado had touched down in it. My feet were dirty from walking barefoot at the river. My new dress was ripped and dirty. Other than swollen red lips and flushed cheeks, my face carried no evidence of Tyler's smack or the kisses and caresses Nick had bandaged it with. There was no outward evidence that my body still pulsed with pleasure from my night with Nick, but it was there, inside me, flowing like lava.

Thinking about Nick and what we had done sent tingles across my entire body. My nipples hardened and strained against my dress. I pulled off my dress and bra and tossed them onto my chair.

Tentatively, my hands moved to my breasts and

teased the points as Nick had done. The look on my face was one of pure bliss. I ran my hands slowly over the rest of my body, imagining it was Nick's hands on me. I slid my hand between my legs and fingered my pussy like he'd done, imagining it was his dick inside me. At the erotic vision of his hot cum shooting on my stomach, I shuddered and came for the third time that night.

Minutes later, after my shower, I was in bed trying to gather my thoughts so I could write in my journal about my night with Nick. A soft knock sounded on my door, and Mom walked in and sat down on the side of my bed.

"Angela, I…" She paused, hesitant, for some reason, to complete her sentence.

"Mom, what is it?" I said impatiently. "You're acting so weird tonight. And it's not just because I came home late."

"Your father and I love you very much, and we only want what's best for you."

I tried not to roll my eyes. I'd heard this preamble a million times. It usually came before their insistence that I do something I didn't want to do. "I know."

"I don't usually pry into your life."

Yeah, right!

"But after tonight, I…"

"What is it you're trying so hard not to say?"

"Did you use protection?"

"Protection?" The word caught in my throat and came out sounding coarse and ugly.

"When you and that boy had sex tonight."

I felt a burning in my stomach like I'd been stabbed, and I wanted to heave from sheer embarrassment.

"Mom! Why would you think we…" I couldn't even say it. I felt a massive twinge of guilt lying to her, but there was no way I was having "the talk" with her tonight right after I'd had sex. That was just way too creepy!

She placed her hand on my journal and kept her eyes downcast to its colorful cover.

Now I realized why she was acting so weird. She had read my vow to "have sex with Nick Spencer if I ever got the chance" and was sure I had kept that vow tonight. Feeling betrayed and violated, I grabbed my journal and held it to my chest in a protective clutch.

"How could you? This is private! I don't go into your room and snoop into your private stuff."

"My only excuse is that you're my daughter and I love you. These days, your journal is the only way I can find out what's happening in your life, what you're thinking and feeling, whether you're happy, when you might be in trouble."

"Have you ever thought about just asking me?" Sarcasm gave my words a bite.

"I do, but you just shut me out. You used to talk to me about your life, your friends, but you haven't done that since you started writing about him. You've grown so secretive, and I don't know what's going on with you." Her voice wavered, and the cherry red flush that had appeared at the tip of her surgically enhanced nose told me she was fighting tears. "I'm worried about you."

A pocket of grief erupted in my heart, and I softened my tone. "I'm not trying to shut you out of my life. I just need some privacy."

"When you love someone, and you've spent years protecting that person, it's hard to let go. It's one of the lessons I'm trying to learn. But, if I see you headed down a path that I know will only bring you pain, my job as a parent, as someone who loves you, is to do or say whatever it takes to help you steer clear of it."

"I'm not a little girl who needs her parents to decide everything for her. I'm making my own choices, my own mistakes, and learning the lessons I need to learn. You can't do it for me. I may not always do the right thing, but you have to trust that I'll come to you if I need help."

Mom paused for a moment, her watery blue eyes holding my steely green ones. "When you came home with that boy tonight, and you said his name, I nearly passed out from fear that you had done something you couldn't undo, something that would ruin your life. I know how you feel about him—you were very clear about it in your journal. But if you didn't use protection or engaged in 'risky' behaviors, let me take you to the gynecologist and get things...taken care of."

"There's no need for that. I promise."

"Okay," she said after a moment and hugged me.

She didn't sound convinced, but I could tell she was going to drop it. Although I was still mad about her invasion of my privacy, I hugged her back.

"You're my brilliant, beautiful daughter, and I love you. But I swear you'll be the death of me before you go off to college." She shifted away but stayed on the bed.

"Why are you so sure I had sex with Nick?"

She reached out and pushed a strand of wet hair away from my face and tucked it behind my ear. "I saw the look on your face, and his, when you ran back to tell him goodbye. How he touched your face, and you clutched his hand."

I said nothing to deny it. I couldn't. She was right. Nick and I looked like we'd had great sex because we had. Warmth flooded through me at the thought.

"It's obvious that you enjoyed each other." She looked pointedly at me, her gaze pinning me to the bed, all humor and light evaporated from her eyes. "He's a very good-looking boy. I can see the attraction. But for both your sakes, it would be best if this were a one-time thing. He's not the kind of guy a girl like you gets involved with. He'll only get hurt. And I'm sure you don't want that."

She paused to let her words sink in then she squeezed my hand, rose from the bed, and left my room, closing the door quietly behind her.

I tried to imagine bringing Nick home to meet my parents, introducing him to the Carringtons, taking him to the country club for dinner. He'd get eaten alive by that crowd, made to feel insignificant. I'd seen it happen before when someone dared to bring in an outsider. I didn't want Nick to go through that.

She was right, I guess.

Being with Nick had been heaven, but as my parents' reactions had reminded me, there were differences between us that couldn't be bridged with great sex. And I wasn't the kind of girl who sneaked around, having a secret affair. Knowing all that didn't stop the sadness from creeping over me when I accepted the fact that I'd never be with Nick again.

I would have to deal with the repercussions of my imprudent behavior on Monday, but for the rest of the weekend, I would replay the scenes of our joining in my mind again and again and enjoy every second. Nick's essence running throughout my body, I turned off the lamp, rolled onto my side, my journal clutched tightly against me, and tried to fall asleep fast. Because in my dreams was the only place I'd get to be with him again.

Chapter Four

I worried all weekend about what I would say to Nick, and what he would say to me, when we saw each other in school. Part of me worried he'd say something and embarrass me in front of my friends, and the other part worried he'd ignore me, making it clear I'd been nothing to him but a one-night stand. I wasn't sure which scenario I'd hate more.

By lunchtime on Monday, I thought maybe I had lucked out of seeing him that day. My stomach was too tied up in knots to eat, but I joined up with my best friend, Gena, and another friend, Olivia, as they headed to the cafeteria.

"What are we doing here?" I asked, my nose wrinkling in distaste. We usually went off campus to where the food was palatable.

"Change of scenery," Olivia said, a smile on her smooth, flawless face.

"She means the football team," Gena added, nodding to the noisy table in the middle of the room, where a dozen team members sat, talking loud, laughing, eating, throwing food.

"Scenery is about all you're going to get in here," I mumbled as we got in line. Gena and Olivia got their trays and plates and moved down the line choosing their lunch. I, however, had to wait for a clean stack of plates, since my friends got the last two.

The new stack finally arrived, hot and wet, and I grabbed one and put it on a tray, sliding it down the metal shelf toward the selection of what could only loosely be described as food. I was frowning between the greasy, cold pizza and fatty, cold burgers, when big, strong hands grasped my hips from behind and the front of a very hard, very male body curled against my backside. Before I could spin around to demand he let me go, a familiar voice whispered next to my ear.

"It would be a shame to ruin such a perfect body with this garbage."

Nick!

As he spoke, his hands moved down and fanned across my lower abdomen. The tips of his long fingers brushed the top of my mound through my skirt, and chills skated the length of my body. I spun around, out of his arms, and faced him, my eyes and face hot.

"Don't do that," I said in a hushed tone, my eyes darting about to see who might have witnessed the display of intimacy.

"Don't do what?" he asked, the heat in his smile and eyes singeing me.

"Touch me like that. People will think we're…" My face grew hotter at my unfortunate choice of words, remembering that any thoughts "people" got would be right on target. Nick had no qualms about putting words to my thought.

"Fucking?"

I felt like I'd swallowed my tongue. "Nick!"

He smiled, clearly amused by my discomfort.

Nodding his head in my friends' direction prompted me to look that way. They were watching us. Damn!

"Did you tell them about us, Angel?" He had leaned in to whisper the sentence into my ear—the very ear he had nibbled a few nights ago—and the feel of his warm cinnamon breath against my skin sent shivers of desire up and down my spine. "Did you tell them what we did to each other? Did you tell them I gave you that hickey on your neck you're trying to hide with makeup and that scarf? Did you tell them about the one on the top of your left breast? The one on your stomach? The one on your right inside thigh, next to your sweet pussy?"

I spun around toward my tray, refusing to meet his eyes, refusing to answer his question, but his brands were pulsing, burning my skin.

"Nah, I didn't think so," he continued. His hands returned to my hips and gripped them, and he turned me around to face him. He meant to take me in his arms, but I stepped, almost jumped, back.

"No!" I seethed, barely above a whisper.

"No, what?" came a voice behind me.

I turned around. The cashier looked at me with more than a hint of annoyance in her beady, heavily lined eyes and her pinched red mouth chewing a wad of gum. I had somehow made it to the end of the line by the cashier, but had absolutely nothing on my plate.

I couldn't go back through the line without further embarrassing myself. My eyes fell to Nick's tray. Somehow, he had chosen a burger and the pizza, two cartons of milk, cookies, and an apple and a banana. He had more than two hands, I decided.

"No," I repeated, "I am not paying for his lunch." I grabbed his apple. "But he's paying for mine."

I glared at Nick and bit hard into the apple.

Leaving my tray in line, I sauntered away toward my friends, the sound of his laughter in my ears and the burning touch of his eyes on my backside.

"What was that about?" Gena began, a grin on her face, when I sat next to her.

"Yeah, he's, like, disgusting for thinking he can talk to you," Olivia chirped in, her nose crinkled.

He's anything but disgusting, I wanted to shout. Instead I betrayed him. "Oh, he was just being a jerk."

Shame washed over me, and I immediately wanted to retract the lie. Gena eyed me like I'd sprouted another nose, but I quickly switched the subject to how horrible the food was. In truth, the apple I'd bitten into tasted like ash in my mouth, through no fault of its own. I could be eating my favorite filet mignon, and it would have tasted as bad.

To get them off the topic of Nick, I fell on my sword and asked Olivia about her summer trip to Bora Bora, which I'd already heard, yawn, three times. It earned me a well-deserved pinch on the leg from Gena.

****

The library was all but deserted when I went in during lunch the next day to find some sources for a presentation. My concentration was on the row of books in front of me, so I didn't see Nick until he stood almost beside me.

He took my notebook and pen from my hands and dropped them to the floor, then took my hands in his, linking our fingers. His eyes tight on mine the whole way, he backed me up until I reached the wall at the end of the aisle. Then he moved even closer and pressed his body against mine, lifting my arms above my head. His cinnamon breath was as soft and erotic as a feather brushing against my lips. My body became electrified at his nearness, my heart pounding so hard I thought it would burst through my rib cage.

"We're going to make love again." He whispered the promise against my lips, and then kissed them. The thought of resisting him evaporated as I melted into the kiss. His tongue plunged into my mouth, tasting me.

The second he released my hands and wrapped his arms around my waist, my arms fastened around his neck and pulled him closer, my moans of delight encouraging him to do more than kiss.

As if he knew my sounds, knew what they meant, his hand slid under my shirt and up my side to cup my breast, and he pressed it, kneaded it, in a slow, circular motion, using his thumb and finger and the lace of my bra to plump my nipple into a bead. My heart melted and rose hot up to my throat, exiting my mouth as soft mewing sounds as I swayed into him, pressing my breast deeper into his palm where it belonged.

Thoughts of where I was, what I was doing, left me. All I knew was that I wanted more of this feeling, more of him. I did want to make love with him again. Right now.

As suddenly as he had captured me, he released me, holding me away from him, looking me up and down, seeing the truth of my feelings all over my body.

"I want you, Angel, and I know you want me," he said, his voice ragged. "But you need to come to me and tell me what you want. And I won't wait forever."

He kept his eyes locked with mine as he backed away. At the end of the aisle, he turned and strode away, leaving me staring dumbly at the vacant place where he had been, my mouth hanging open, my heart still pounding a rapid fire in my throat, my body still pulsing with desire.

If I'd had the slightest breath left, I would have called him back and asked him to make love to me right there. But then I remembered the reality of our situation. Yes, we wanted each other, but it would never work between us beyond an occasional blissful fuck. Hell, I couldn't even talk to him with my friends around.

It was time to settle this between us, like adults, and I would do it after school.

My car was in the shop so I'd ridden to school with Gena. I told her I was staying late to do some research in the library and to go on home without me. After she and the rest of my friends left, I looked for Nick and found him at the motorcycle parking spots, packing up to go. Fortunately, he was alone.

I glanced around, not seeing anyone but maintenance guys blowing the leaves off the sidewalk several yards away. Taking a deep breath and releasing it, I approached him, vowing to resist his irresistible charms.

"We need to talk." I congratulated myself on sounding sure and strong.

"Hello, Angel." His sexy voice and smile melted my resolve on contact like a flame to a sheet of ice. Green eyes swept across my body, touching off a heat wave in its wake. "I wondered how long it would take." He strapped his backpack to the back of the seat.

"How long what would take?" I snapped.

"To come to me and admit you want a repeat performance of the other night."

My scoffing laughter sounded hollow and fake

even to my ears. He had cut through all my denials, hitting the truth right on the head in one try.

"You certainly have an over-inflated opinion of your performance."

"I made you scream my name and come. Twice. I'd say that was a damn fine performance."

He was so right, but I wasn't ready to give in. "You need to stop this," I said, and swallowed hard.

"Stop what?"

"Everything—the looks, the words, the touches, the…the kisses." *Oh God, the kisses.*

He laughed and said my name, drawing it out like a whispered prayer. "You don't want me to stop. You like what we did. You like *me* doing it to you. And you want to do it again. I can read your face and your body as easy as you read texts on that fancy phone of yours." He fingered the side phone pocket of the backpack hanging on my shoulder.

I shrugged away his touch. "You know nothing about me."

"I know how you like to be kissed. And touched. And fucked. I know how you smell." His voice grew lower and more suggestive. "How you taste—your mouth, your nipples, your skin…"

His words thrilled me to my core and made my breath catch in a shuddering gasp. I was shaking I wanted him so bad. "Leave me alone, Nick. I won't tell you again."

I tried to leave, but he caught me and pulled me to him. He pushed my backpack off my shoulder to the ground, then cupped my ass and pulled me hard up against him, grinding his rigid prick into my pussy. The heated spot between my legs responded eagerly to his suggestion with trickling wetness. My palms flattened helplessly against his chest to try to deny him.

"I don't want this, Nick. I don't want you. I don't. Please." The voice that came out of my mouth was a low, pleading whisper—not to stop, but to ignore my foolish words.

His eyes burned across my face. "Kiss me, Angel. Just once. If you can tell me you don't want me after that, I'll leave you alone. Forever. And we'll forget what happened between us. Otherwise, I'm going to take you somewhere, right now, and fuck you again with the monster cock you begged for the other night."

I swallowed. I blinked. And then with a groan I closed the gap between us and claimed his mouth, making it clear which one I wanted him to do. My arms went around his neck in a fierce grip, and I deepened the kiss, meeting and matching each swirl and thrust of his tongue.

One arm roped around my waist, pulling me closer into him. His hand splayed in my hair, gripping it to hold my head close and my mouth closer to his. He claimed my mouth, claimed me, his head slanting to better possess me, his tongue sparring with mine.

I ground my pussy against his hard bulge to try to find some relief, and he pressed into me with a muffled groan that made it clear he needed relief too. We needed each other. The feel of his chest pressed against my nipples had brushed them into tight, high tips ready for his mouth to devour. Small, breathless grunts escaped from my throat and mingled with his. There was no going back. I was dizzy with the need to be one with him, and I knew we had to finish this dance or die.

I couldn't react like this and deny my true feelings.

My body had hungered for his for days. He was right. I wanted him. Everything about him filled my mind with colorful, intoxicating bubbles, making me forget all but the feelings of the moment. I would have gone anywhere with him, done anything with him at this moment.

I broke the kiss but kept my mouth on his. "Take me somewhere," I said thickly. "Now."

He didn't waste time asking if I was sure. A man of action, he released me, grabbed my backpack and slipped it around my shoulders, and mounted his bike. I climbed on behind him without being asked. He handed me his helmet, and I put it on. He started the beast.

I wrapped my arms around his waist, my legs alongside his hips, and cupped my body to his back. "Go fast," I said, dropping one hand between his legs to squeeze his bulge. "Go really fast."

"I always do," he said, his voice rough, urgent through his sexy grin.

Kicking the bike into gear, he maneuvered it out of the parking lot and down the road that took us away from the school and toward the river. And damn if he didn't keep his word to go fast.

The bike rolled to a stop at our spot, and we both jumped off. He quickly pushed it inside the mouth of our undergrowth cave and tossed his jacket to the ground while I did the same to the helmet and my backpack. He pulled a rolled blanket from the compartment under the seat and spread it on the ground. We flew into each other's arms, and he lowered me to the blanket, pushed up my skirt, and settled between my spread thighs. Every movement of his rotating hips ground his denim-covered erection into me, scraping my panties-covered clit into a frenzy.

"I want to hear you say it, Angel," he whispered, dropping kisses on my face, grinding my pussy, thrusting at my core, pulling the truth from me.

It was daylight. I knew he would be able to see the naked desire in my eyes, and I felt embarrassed by it. I needed time to remove the mask from my face and let Angel come forward. As his Angel, I was free to be the person I was. As his Angel, I had wings that took me to heights of great pleasure. As his Angel, I wasn't controlled by Angela's conditioning. Being Angel was frightening and exhilarating. And he knew just how to call her to get her to come out.

"Say it," he repeated, kissing my mouth, my neck, while his hand roamed over my breasts, pinching the nipples, then slid between us to caress the throbbing heat between my legs. At his touch, Angela vanished and Angel lay in his arms. And without a trace of shyness or hesitation, I gave him what he wanted.

"Did you bring more than one condom this time?"

He sat up and dug into one of his pockets and pulled out three condoms, dropping them on the blanket by my side.

"Then make love to me, Nick."

He yanked his shirt over his head and tossed it aside, while I arched up and pulled off my shirt and removed my bra. His hands went to the snap and zipper of my skirt and yanked it down and off my legs. My hands flew to his jeans and quickly unbuttoned and unzipped him, shoving down his jeans and his boxers. He kicked out of the encumbering clothes, the motion taking his boots and socks too. I grabbed a condom and ripped it open, rolling it on the hard length of him. Our movements were quick and deft, like we'd done this a million times. No trembling hands, no bumping into each other, just smooth, synced motions that got the job done.

I wanted him now, my wet pussy was ready to welcome him, but he moved down, his head between my legs, and mouthed my pussy through my panties.

I grabbed his hair. "No, we can't." He sucked on my pussy, his teeth nipping me, his tongue plunging in as much as my panties barrier would allow, trying to give us both what we needed. It felt really good, but I wanted to feel his cock inside me, deep and filling, making me come apart.

"Nick. I need you now." I bucked into his mouth. "Come inside me."

He sucked my panties-covered clit into his mouth again for a few glorious seconds before yanking the scrap of lacy material off. He put his hand to my pussy and dipped a finger inside me, making me cry out in joy. He stroked me a few times then withdrew it and put that finger in his mouth, sucking my juice from it. It was the most erotic thing I'd ever seen. It pulled from me the most erotic word I knew.

"Oh, fuck. Nick. Fuck me."

He scrambled up my body and sheathed his steel rod inside my needy pussy in one swift stroke. His mouth crushed mine, and we fed off each other, our tongues fucking to the rhythm of our bodies.

The need rose higher in my body every second, every stroke, every thrust, ready to crack and spill over at any time. Feeling him so tight and deep inside me, hearing the sounds of our fucking, feeling his jagged breaths on me, pulling the scent of him into my lungs triggered the spill. I cried out his name as my core clenched around him, and I rode the tsunami of pleasure.

He must have come at the same time because when I came back into my body I could feel him twitching inside me. I felt the tight muscles in his stomach contracting and releasing. Felt him trembling, like he'd given me all of him in the explosive ejection.

My breath was labored, but I pressed my lips to his forehead, his closed eyes, his cheeks, his full, delicious lips. "I missed you. So much."

His eyes opened half way, found mine. "You can have me whenever you want. Just ask."

"You'll have the condoms ready?"

"Always."

****

The first rays of the setting sun were dipping their toes into the shimmering water by the time we'd used those two other condoms, and then Nick and I headed home. We pulled to a stop in front of my house, my Angela mask firmly in place. There would be no lingering kisses or caresses this time, not while there was enough light out for my parents and neighbors to see us.

I scrambled off the bike, removed the helmet he insisted I wear, and stood beside him, awkward and embarrassed, wanting more than anything to bolt into the house without having to have the coming conversation.

"No long goodbye kisses this time?" His voice carried a teasing tone, but I knew my cold behavior bothered him.

I shrugged and tucked my bed-hair behind one ear.

"I'm sure my mom heard the bike drive up." In truth, she was probably watching from the window. "And if she saw us kiss, I'd have to go through this long explanation of why I'm with you again." Actually, she'd know why. "And why hasn't she met you, and—"

"No problem." He cut the engine and looked like he was going to rock the bike on its stand and dismount.

"What are you doing?" I asked, panic in my voice at what Nick seemed to have in mind.

"Going in to meet your mom and explain why you're with me."

His words stole the air from my lungs. The panic racing through my body was seconds from exploding out the top of my head.

"No! I mean...this really isn't a good time. She's already going to be upset because I wasn't home right after school and didn't let her know where I was. Another time."

He sat back down.

"You understand...right?" I said.

"I understand fine."

His stare was blank, his eyes holding no life, no spark. Even his voice seemed flat, as if he were trying to deny the presence of emotions hammering against his insides. If I had to pin down an emotion controlling him, I'd say it was hurt or disappointment, maybe even anger. I had just given him my whole self again and was now rejecting him, again. That couldn't feel good.

I hated to hurt him, but I wasn't sure I was strong enough to go against my parents and my friends and the society I'd grown up in for him—a guy I didn't really know. They wouldn't understand the feelings I had for him. But how could they when I didn't even understand them? They certainly wouldn't understand why we'd never even had one date, or why I'd never mentioned him in family conversations, but I'd had sex with him several times.

Why couldn't he be content with a no-strings relationship where he didn't have to meet the parents? Most guys would die for a setup like that. But then, Nick wasn't like most guys.

"Good. Okay. Well, thanks for the ride home," I said, trying to inject my words with a breezy tone as if I hadn't just crushed his heart with my bare hands like a ripe tomato.

He took the helmet from me and with a shake of his head pulled it on. He started the bike and kicked it into gear. And without a word or look, he sped off.

I dodged the inevitable bullet one more time—my mom wasn't even home. And as I went upstairs to shower Nick from my body, I told myself that for the sake of his heart and mine, he and I would not have sex again.

****

"Oh, frailty, thy name is woman!" I'd heard that line in English class. Shakespeare. And it described my willpower to a T: Weak. Two days later, I asked Nick to make love to me again. And the day after that. And the Monday after that.

I was consumed with thoughts of him. All the time. When we weren't together, I was reliving every detail of every second with him and longing for him, planning the next time we could be together. I was beginning to think I was addicted to him, to sex. Our lovemaking was hot and pleasurable, and he had opened up so many new experiences and feelings for me.

Every time we were together, we made love at least twice. The first was a mad rush to fuck, to take the edge off our hunger to be one; the second was slower, an opportunity to make love, to get to know each other's bodies and needs and sounds, to experiment and to explore other positions—we'd tried four so far: him on top, me on top, me on his lap sitting up, and me on all fours, my ass up to accept him from behind. And we'd talk too. About everything...except our relationship.

After two weeks of being together, he brought me a paper that showed he was clean. No STDs. That day I took his cock into my mouth for the first time. I had never done that with Tyler—or with any guy. It had never appealed to me. But I wanted to experience everything with Nick, and I liked that he enjoyed it so much, as much as I did.

That same day, he made me come with his tongue, no panties in the way. He'd told me he didn't need proof that I was STD free, that my word was enough, but two weeks later I brought him a paper that showed I was clean too.

I loved everything we did. He did too, but he soon made it clear he wanted more. Not more sex. More from our relationship. He wanted to go public, hang out at school, hold hands and kiss at school, go out on dates, meet the parents; basically, he wanted the relationship trappings.

But no matter how much I craved him, I couldn't be with him openly. We ran in different circles. My friends were from well-to-do families and were into shopping, parties, and preparing to get into the best colleges, marriages, and social organizations. My friends and family wouldn't understand my attraction for him any more than his friends, whoever they were, would accept his feelings for what they would call a snobby, spoiled, preppy bitch.

I had to come up with a solution to this problem. Fast. I couldn't be out with him, but I certainly couldn't be without him.

We had yet another argument about it the day we ditched class after lunch to spend more time together at the river. We lay naked on our blanket, me tucked into his side, contented and satiated, trailing my fingers lightly across his skin.

"Go to the movies with me Friday night," he said.

I stilled, tensed. "Thanks, but I can't."

He stilled, tensed too. "Why not?"

I rose up and dug a piece of gum from his jeans pockets so I wouldn't have to meet his eyes.

He rose up too. "Why are we hiding our relationship?"

"I love being with you, Nick. You know that. But I don't want to share you or what we have with anyone." I put the stick of cinnamon gum in my mouth.

"What you mean is that being seen with me would ruin your perfectly arranged image, so you want us to sneak around."

It impressed me how quickly he had seen through my veil of half-truths to the coil of fear in my heart. I tried to explain. "What I mean is that I want us to enjoy each other without all the drama of unfolding a relationship in front of everyone. We don't need that."

"That's bullshit." Anger dripped from his words. "Either we're all in, or we're out. Decide. Now."

When I didn't respond, he grabbed his boxers. But before he could stand to put them on, I yanked them from his hands and held them between my breasts to keep him from leaving.

"Nick, listen—"

"I've heard all I want to hear." He yanked them out of my hands and tried to stand again, but I grabbed him by his dick. A mean, but necessary, trick to get him to stay put. It caught him off guard, enabling me to grab his boxers and toss them out of his reach, unless he stood and walked to them.

"Look, maybe I didn't explain it right," I began, but he interrupted.

"No, you explained it really well. You want my cock, but not the rest of me."

"That's not at all what I said. Or what I meant. Or what I want."

He put his hand on mine and tried to gently remove my hand from his member. "Let go," he seethed.

Determined that he hear me out, I tightened my grip, and my hand around him became more purposeful in its movements. I enjoyed the spark of victory when I felt it lengthening and thickening in my hand. And when he wasn't still trying to get away, I slowed down, wanting to show him why we couldn't do anything to risk losing this thing between us.

He sat with his legs out and spread, and now he leaned back on his hands, giving me full access to the most vulnerable part of his body. My one hand went to his balls and caressed them gently, massaged them, while the other hand gripped tightly at the base of his shaft. I stroked slowly upward, taking time to round my palm over his cockhead, juicing the wetness from him.

Without warning, I leaned over and put my mouth on him. A startled little moan of appreciation preceded his hips pressing up slightly, pressing his cock deeper into my mouth, showing me he liked what I was doing. My lips rode up and down his rigid cock, my tongue swirling over his heavy cockhead, tasting his slight tang and swallowing it hungrily.

Again and again, I licked and stroked him, my lips tight and wet on him, until he was throbbing with need, his lungs heaving to draw in enough air. A long, low animal sound groaned from his body and made his stomach draw tight.

Feeling him warm and hard and pulsing in my mouth sent a rush of power through me that I could make him feel such pleasure. I glanced up at his face. His eyes were at half mast, his full lips parted to take in more oxygen, his stomach muscles jerking now and then when I sucked hard, my cheeks hollowing out. Seeing the desire on his face, hearing his moans, smelling and tasting his cum and mine from before, feeling him so hard and ready again, reminded me that my core was throbbing too. I had to have him.

I pulled back, his cock popping from my mouth wet and hard, and grabbed a condom from the blanket. I rolled it on him, then climbed onto his lap. He sat up and gripped my hips, his fingers digging in, his whole body hardening against me, tense from wanting.

I wrapped my arms around his neck, my legs around his waist. A slight shift upward had me poised over his erection. I slid onto him, slowly, making sure he felt every layer of sweet friction we created together, until he filled me completely, touched the very top of me. A muffled groan rose from his chest the deeper he went, and his head fell backward, his eyes closed, his teeth gritting at the feeling.

Rocking up and down, back and forth, on him, I kept my eyes on his face where I could see his desire for me, could see whether my actions were having an effect.

He felt so good inside me, I could hardly speak. I didn't want to speak. I only wanted to feel, to move, to bring us both to completion. But I had to speak until I'd convinced him not to do what he should do, which was tell me to go to hell and never have another thing to do with me.

"Baby, if they…" Oh, God, this was hard. This talking thing. My brain had shut down to all but basic functions like breathing and feeling. Rational thought wasn't one of them, but I fought through the fog. He had to hear me. "If others know, they'll cause trouble for us," I whispered against his mouth. "They'll take me away from you. And I don't think I can live without you."

His eyes found mine. His pupils were wide and dark in his liquid green eyes. His full, luscious lips softened and parted on a groan of a response. But I wasn't sure he was hearing anything I was saying. His hands gripped my hips tighter, his hips bucked higher and faster, stabbing harder into my core, encouraging me to ride him faster. Squeezing my thighs on his, I fought to maintain the slower pace, wanting to draw it out, make it memorable.

As if he'd had enough of foreplay, his hands gripping my hips went around my waist and back in a tight grip, and he lowered me down, onto my back, him right on me, and took control. His mouth came down on mine, and with sharp, fast grunts slammed his hips against me, again and again, his cock inside me growing harder and longer.

My legs went higher, opened wider, to give him all of me. We grunted and groaned and bucked, sweat sealing our bodies together in a fantastic battle. He tensed inside me, then growled, his head back, his eyes squeezed shut. Sawing in and out in earnest, he found his release. I could feel the heat of his cum filling the condom. His last few thrusts pulled me over with him. My pussy opened and released, and I came around him, my orgasm stroking out the last of his.

Shaking with his release, Nick clutched me to him. I tasted the salty sweat on his brow when I kissed him there. I felt his heart kicking against my chest. I heard his lungs pulling in air to keep his hold on life. I felt his cock twitching inside me, his stomach muscles spasm. I smelled the haze of our orgasm rising hot and thick from our skin like summer heat off a blacktop.

His mouth hovered over mine, each giving the other breaths we couldn't seem to find on our own. We were still blind, our heads still spinning, our bodies still melding, trying to hold onto that magical moment when two became one. But I found a way to speak.

"Can you give this up?"

I wondered what answer I'd see in his eyes when he found the strength to open them, what he'd say when he had breath enough to speak. Wondered whether this would be our last time together.

His eyes slowly opened half way, found mine. I had my answer, but I had to make sure. "Please, Nick. Do it this way for me. For us. For now." The words whispered out, my mouth too dry to speak in a normal voice.

"For now, Angel. But not for long. I'm tired of

being your dirty little secret."

And then he kissed me, softly this time, and I forgot about everything but the touch of his hand, the taste of his mouth, the feel of his body.

Chapter Five

A few days after Nick had reluctantly agreed to my terms, Gena and I were sitting in the senior commons talking when I felt eyes on me. My skin warmed as if caressed by a loving hand. I glanced around and saw Nick at his locker. He nodded slightly in greeting, then winked. My heart flipped, and I bit back a smile at the heat in his eyes, at the tip of his talented tongue licking his full bottom lip.

I wanted to rush into his arms, take that tongue in my mouth, then kiss him all the way to class, holding his hand. But instead I stayed planted in my seat. Watching him and only half listening to my friend, I didn't notice Tyler until he plopped down in the foot-wide space between Gena and me, knocking us both aside.

"Tyler! What the hell?" I shot him a hateful look.

"Hey, babe." Before I could scoot away from him, he put his arm around my shoulder and kissed me.

"Asshole!" I seethed, jumping up and away from him as quickly as I could, wiping his kiss from my mouth.

"Shit, good to see you too," Tyler replied dryly, his frown showing that my reaction had annoyed him.

I grabbed my backpack and let my eyes dart to Nick. His hands were clenched in fists, and his face was a mask of fury. He looked so tightly wound that he'd spring if anyone breathed on him.

"Gena, let's get to bio early so we can get a seat together."

Gena stared wide-eyed at us, trying to figure out what was going on. I could understand her confusion. The only details I'd shared with her about my breakup with Tyler were that we'd had broken up. I certainly hadn't shared any details about my relationship with Nick.

"Gena?" I prompted to shake her out of her fog.

"Uh, yeah." She jumped up and grabbed her bag.

We had to walk past Nick on our way out of the commons. I could tell he was upset, and when I gave him a small smile as we passed, he didn't smile back. Right before I exited the door, I heard his locker slam.

"Okay, that was weird," Gena said as we were walking down the path to bio. "What is up with you guys?"

"I told you, I broke up with him."

"I mean with you and Nick."

She didn't say, "Duh," but it was there in her surprised voice.

"What are you talking about?" I said innocently, grateful I hadn't fallen on my face when I stumbled over my feet at her sentence.

"Don't play innocent with me. I saw the looks passing between you two. The heat almost singed my eyelashes. And he looked like he was going to strangle Tyler when he kissed you."

I rolled my eyes to dismiss her claims. "I don't know what you think you saw, but I'm telling you there's nothing…I don't even know him."

Gena grabbed my arm and stopped me. "Angie."

I looked at her. "What?"

"If something is going on between you two, you better make sure Tyler doesn't find out."

"Why?"

"Remember how you sat next to Kyle Jonah in Spanish class yesterday?"

At my nod, she continued. "I heard that Tyler shoved him up against the cafeteria wall outside and threatened to 'rearrange his face for him' if Kyle ever sat next to 'my girl' again. Kyle came to econ with a red blotch on his face, like he'd been punched."

My eyebrows lowered into a frown. "I sat next to Kyle because I was late and that was the only empty seat," I explained.

"Yeah, I know that. Just think what Tyler'll do if he suspects you and Nick are doing more than just giving each other fuck-me-now looks."

"I told you, we're not—"

"Why are you lying to me?" She sliced through my lie, hurt and anger in her tone.

"Gena, I'm not," I said, feeling like a bitch for lying to my best friend.

She shook her head and rolled her eyes. "Whatever. Just warn him."

"Warn who?"

I spun around. Tyler stood behind us, suspicion hardening his face.

God, I hoped he hadn't heard us say Nick's name. Ignoring him, I linked my arm with Gena's and led her down the path. Tyler moved in front of us, not letting us pass.

"Warn who?" He stuck his face in Gena's face.

"Warn you to brush your teeth a little more often,"

she said, stepping back and waving her hand in front of her nose. "Dude, your breath smells like ass."

He smiled like a wolf about to devour a sheep. "You're funny, bitch."

"C'mon, Gena." I stepped between them and again linked her arm with mine and pulled her away toward a group of teachers who were walking down the path. Tyler didn't follow us, but I felt him staring after us.

I'd warn Nick during lunch.

****

After class started, I got a pass to go to the restroom so I could rush back to the commons and leave a note in Nick's locker asking him to meet me at lunch. We had met a few times in the grove of trees past the soccer field to make out, especially on those days he had to go to work right after school—like today—and couldn't go somewhere to make love.

I'd been pacing and gritting my teeth for nearly five minutes when I saw him running toward me. He had such a smooth athletic gait, like running was as easy as breathing for him. Just watching his body in motion dissolved my anger and made me wish we were at a more secluded spot.

"You're late," I said, my tone chilling the words to ice cubes. I wasn't that mad, but I couldn't let him think he could make me wait all the time.

He grinned and pulled me into his embrace.

I kept my arms crossed and my mouth averted.

"You need to get a cell phone," I said, frost still dusting my voice, "so I can text you instead of leaving you stupid little notes."

"Cell phones are for spoiled rich kids, not poor working kids like me. C'mon, give me some love, spoiled rich kid." His lips snuggled against mine and his hand cupped my breast.

"You think I called you here just so you could feel me up?" I teased.

"Yes."

In truth, I hadn't called him for any other reason but to warn him about Tyler, but now that he was here pressed against me, setting fires inside me, having his body ravage mine was the only thing on my mind. The remaining icicles of anger melted in the heat of his touch.

I met his eyes with a wicked grin. "Got a problem with that?"

His hands went to my blouse and unbuttoned it, undid the front hook on my bra and moved it aside, revealing my breasts. He cupped both breasts, playing his thumbs across my nipples like a tight guitar string.

"What do you think?" he said.

Before I could answer, he dipped his head and put his mouth over my nipple, sucking so deep I felt a tug in my womb. The flames raging in my body burned away my oxygen supplies. I held his head against me.

"Ahh, Nick. Do you know what you do to me?"

"The same thing you do to me," he whispered into my skin and sucked the other lucky nipple into his mouth. "Make me feel alive."

Had two people ever been more sexually compatible than Nick and me? I couldn't get enough. He spoiled me. Found new ways to make me feel good, and I did the same for him.

His hand slid up my skirt, and his fingers played between my legs, inside my panties, while his mouth stayed to play with my nipples.

"Let's get out of here," he said in between licks.

The "no" forming on my tongue felt like a burr. "Class starts soon. No way can we get there and back in time."

"We could if you didn't insist on coming three times."

I gently pushed him away and refastened my bra. "Are you calling me greedy?"

Other than a laugh, he didn't respond. He stopped my hands from buttoning my shirt and put his hands on my breasts. He loved my breasts. He'd said so just yesterday. He'd spent an inordinate amount of time on them and when I commented on it, he laughed and said, *I fucking love your tits. They're the most beautiful, delicious tits in the world, and they're all mine. I can't get enough of them.*

"If I am greedy, it's your fault," I said.

He slid from my arms, a grin on his face. "Guess we'll have to wait then. Until we have more time. Maybe next week."

I yanked him back to me and wrapped my leg around his hip to let him know that I wouldn't wait, couldn't wait.

"No, not next week. Now. Meet me in the parking lot in two minutes."

"I have to get my backpack, so make it five." He kissed me hard on the mouth. "I can't wait to eat your pussy." He slid the words onto my lips and kissed them in, then released me, turned, and ran back the way he'd come. On unsteady legs, I rushed toward the parking lot, buttoning my blouse as I went, determined to destroy anything or anyone who got in my way.

I stepped into the parking lot and raced for my car,

unlocking the doors with the key fob as I did. I had my hand on the door when I felt a hand on my shoulder. I spun around, my heart pounding a hole in my chest.

"Afternoon, Ms. Abbott."

Headmaster Daniel Wilson stood behind me, a question in the smile on his face.

"Oh! Mr. Wilson." I like to think I recovered pretty quickly, but by the concerned look on his face, I think I looked as guilty as I felt. "I didn't see you there."

"I startled you."

I laughed and tossed my backpack into the backseat. "I'm starving, so I wasn't paying attention to anything but getting out of here for some lunch."

He checked his watch, and I knew he was going to comment that my class was starting in thirty-five minutes, leaving me little time to get lunch and get back. My brain went into overdrive trying to think of something to distract him.

"Uh, how's Ming?"

A smile expanded on his face, and I knew I'd hit on the right dodge. Everyone knew about Mr. Wilson's great love for his dogs, especially his new pug puppy.

"Ming? Oh, she's a joy. I taught her to shake hands last night."

I hoped my chuckle didn't sound as fake to him as it felt to me. "Already? She's a fast learner."

His face clouded over for a moment, and I thought I was in for it.

"You know the wife and I weren't blessed with our own children. So our dogs are everything to us."

In the pause that followed, he looked so wistful I felt something other than desire and deception gnawing at my stomach.

"You'd have made a terrific father, Mr. Wilson. You're so patient and understanding."

That seemed to please him because he brightened again. "Well, I don't know about that, but thank you, Angela. You're kind for saying so."

I smiled.

"Okay, now get on to lunch so you can get back in time for your next class."

"I will," I called to his retreating form, just as Nick ran across the quad toward the parking lot. Mr. Wilson called out to him, stopping him. I couldn't hear their exchange, but I understood the conversation by their motions.

Nick looked toward the parking lot. Mr. Wilson shook his head. Nick shook his head, then lowered his backpack to the cement, unzipped it, and pulled out a folded piece of paper. Mr. Wilson pulled it out of his hand, unfolded it, read it thoroughly as if looking for problems, then tossed it back toward him. It fell to the ground. Nick picked it up, refolded it, and returned it to his backpack. Mr. Wilson said some parting words, complete with finger pointing, and stormed away toward the administration building.

Nick continued on his way to the lot at a furious pace. His face was a thundercloud of emotion. He passed my car with barely a look in my direction and walked toward the road.

Where was he going on foot? I jumped into my car and soon pulled up next to him, rolling down the window.

"Nick. Get in."

He kept walking, his body stiff like a soldier on a march, his eyes focused on unseen enemies ahead.

One eye on the road, one on Nick, I called to him again. "Nick, please. I need you."

"I'm the last person you need," he yelled. "Just go back to your world, Angela. You don't belong in mine any more than I belong in yours."

I gunned it and pulled off the road in front of him, jumping out of the car and going to him, grabbing his arm.

"What happened with Wilson?" I demanded, though I already knew.

He pulled free of my grip and moved away. "It doesn't matter."

I stepped in front of him again and wrapped my arms around his waist.

"It matters to me." I kissed him.

He didn't move away, but his statue-like stance didn't bend, his tight mouth stayed firm.

"You matter to me." I kissed him again. And again.

I soon felt his lips go soft, warm, and kiss me back. Felt his rigid posture relax against me as he curled his arms around me.

These kisses felt different somehow than any other kisses we'd shared. They weren't hot like those that drove us to this point. They weren't playful, like so many times before. They went deeper, made me feel comforted and comfortable, like we'd buried ourselves together beneath a fuzzy blanket on a snowy morning and were keeping each other warm.

I felt connected to him in a way I hadn't been before. Understanding passed between us, and it was a feeling I'd never experienced with any other guy I'd cared about. It was real. He did matter to me. He was mine. And I felt a gripping need to protect him.

Yeah, these feelings were real, but they scared me. Every minute with him pushed me toward a decision I didn't want to make. But right now, I wanted him, and I would have him.

I pulled back slightly, smiled. "Get in the car, Spencer. You promised me some lovin'." I took his hand and led him to the car.

The road leading down to the riverbank was still muddy from the rain the night before, and I didn't want to chance getting my car stuck. The explanations would be impossible. I suggested we go to a movie and sit at the very top row. He suggested something else.

I pulled into the driveway of a house that would fit into my garage. The red brick walls were bordered with tan plastic siding. Windows, though small, were dirt- and spider-web free and, unlike some of the neighboring homes, had screens that were intact and in place. A little patch of grass grew inside a rectangular border of thick railroad ties, and a couple of squat bushes with yellow flowers guarded the front door. It was old and used, with a favorite-old-pair-of-jeans feeling to it, and so different from my own home.

Nick unlocked the front door and pushed it open for me. I stood on the three-foot wide cement porch as motionless as the potted plants next to me, nervous about going inside. He took my hand and kissed my palm. His other hand went to my waist.

"C'mon. Let's go in."

My feet felt like part of the cement. "Are you sure this is okay?" I looked behind me as if someone was watching me.

"Yeah, Mom hid the drugs and bodies before she went to work."

My stomach dropped to my knees, and it felt like my eyes were bugging out. He laughed.

Up to that point, I had my backpack tight against my chest, both hands holding onto it. When I realized he was making fun of me, I rapped him with it.

"Oh, you are so not funny."

"If you'd seen your face, you'd laugh too. You were scared to death."

"No, I wasn't."

Doubt lifted his eyebrows, and he shook his head.

"I wasn't," I insisted firmly.

"My mistake," he said, one corner of his luscious mouth tipped up in a controlled grin.

I stepped through the door and took in the details of the neat, clean, fresh-smelling room. Light filled the space through tied-back sheer curtains. I set my backpack down on the coffee table. Not a speck of dust blemished its scarred but polished surface, or the matching lamp table, or the table that held an old, pre-flat-screen TV a couple of feet deep.

A colorful hand-crocheted throw covered the back of the faded gold and green plaid couch. Two chairs flanked it, one a rocker in a bumpy oatmeal fabric and the other a recliner in brown faux leather. All pointed toward the TV as if it were the prime entertainment.

If TV was king, the short, wide, tilting bookcase stuffed with books suggested that reading was a close second. The weight of the books—textbooks, romances, comics, children's books, literary classics, mysteries, and ragged best sellers from years ago—swayed the pressboard shelves. I could almost hear it groan.

As I looked around, I couldn't help but compare it to my home, with its separate living room, den, study/library areas; a laundry room the size of this living room; five bedrooms, each with its own bathroom and sitting area and walk-in closet; a gourmet kitchen with eat-in breakfast nook; formal dining room, and so much more that I felt embarrassed even thinking about it.

I liked Nick. A lot. And the sex was mind-blowing. But seeing his house, seeing him in his world, stripped away all my rainbows and blue skies to reveal how very different our worlds were.

Not that I needed a guy who could give me fancy gifts and take me on expensive dates to be happy—Tyler had given me the best gifts money could buy, and I had been miserable. But I wasn't sure my character was strong enough not to care that any dates with Nick would mostly be hanging out somewhere that didn't cost money. Or not to cringe in guilt every time he pulled hard-earned singles from his wallet to pay for our meal at some fast food place—I know his pride would not allow me to pay. Or not to care that my parents would absolutely flip at the thought of their daughter, their only child, getting involved with a guy who had this present and a likely similar future considering he probably wasn't going to college.

What am I doing with him? Panic squirreled through me at the thought. I should end this game we were playing before we both got hurt.

I was about to suggest that we go back to school when my gaze fell on two metal frames hanging on the wall above the bookcase. I walked over to them. One held a school photo of a young boy of about six or seven who resembled Nick but with blond hair and eyes so dark they looked black. The other photo was of Nick, a younger Nick, maybe twelve or thirteen, in a red and black football uniform.

He hadn't put his tough on yet. The smile that these days usually just peeked out at one corner took up the entire mouth and lit his eyes. A dark sweep of bangs stuck up from his forehead, like he'd wiped sweat from them just before the picture was snapped. The emotions in his green eyes were close to the surface, there for all to see, not hidden as they were in the older Nick I knew. I ran my finger across the handsome face, wishing I'd known this carefree and happy boy.

Behind me, Nick wrapped his arms around my waist.

I leaned back against him, put my hands on his. "What position did you play?"

He nudged aside my hair and kissed my neck. "Wide receiver."

"Ahh, which means you were fast."

"And had good hands," he said and slid one of his talented hands to my breast and cupped it.

"That hasn't changed," I said with a chuckle as his fingers pinched my nipple into a bead. "When was this taken? How old were you?"

"Twelve. Almost thirteen."

His other hand slid under my skirt, between my legs, and into my panties.

"You looked happy," I said.

He teased my clit with the tip of one finger. "It was taken just before my dad—"

He chopped off whatever words he was going to say as if he had just realized he was letting something slip. His hands fell away from my body.

I turned to face him. "Before your dad what?" I slid

my arms around his waist.

After a moment, he answered, but he was looking at the picture, not at me. "Left."

A fist twisted in my heart at the pain he must have endured at the breakup of his family. "Baby, I'm sorry."

He took a step back out of my arms, then two. "Hey, shit happens."

I could see him clouding over, disconnecting from me, but I kept pushing, wanting to know this thing about him that he so didn't want to share. I had a feeling the sharing would bring us closer.

"An affair?" I asked.

He nodded, his face tight, and shifted back another step.

I stepped forward one step. "Do you see him much—"

His entire body tensed like a statue, and his eyes bored into mine. "Do you want to talk or do you want to fuck? We don't have time to do both."

His words stung like a slap. I stood there for a stunned moment, paralyzed by his anger and his crudeness. Clearly I had touched a nerve asking about his father. And instead of talking about it, which was obviously too painful, or asking me to back off, he struck out to hurt me to get me to step off.

I shook my head and grabbed his hand. "Don't do that. Not to me."

He moved away from me, wouldn't look me in the eye. "Do what?"

"Push me away for wanting to know about the important things in your life."

"I came here to fuck, not play Ten Questions."

I stood there, shaking with anger, both from his

words and that he didn't trust me enough to share something personal about his life with me. I lunged forward and shoved him in the chest so hard he rocked back a few more steps.

His eyes were tight on me. His mouth was a tight line. His hands were in tight fists, and the rest of his body was just as tight.

I reached up under my skirt and yanked my panties off, throwing them at his face. He snatched them out of the air with one hand and balled them in his fist.

I walked the few steps backward until my back met the wall. I spread my legs and raised my skirt high, exposing myself to him. "Is this what you came for? Is this all you want from me?"

Lust flared in his eyes as his gaze licked over my bare pussy, and it surged through his body so hot and fast I could almost smell it, like smoke from a fire. The look on his face said his answer was a resounding yes.

"Then come and get it, you son of a bitch," I said, my voice sharp, angry, full of challenge. "Fuck me."

He dropped my panties to the floor and his hands flew to his jeans. Jerking open the stud and zipper, he shoved his jeans and boxers down just enough to free his cock. All eight inches of it jutted hard and angry and pulsing into the charged air between us, and he fisted it like a sword. He pulled a condom from his pocket, ripped it open with his teeth, and stormed forward, toward me, rolling the condom on his rock-hard shaft as he did.

He slammed his body into mine, making the wall shake. "Why the fuck not? This is all you want from me." The sharp, angry words gritted through his clenched teeth.

He bent down and with his arms hooked my spread legs at my thighs, lifting me up, opening me up. My body tilted back at the quick motion, causing my head to bang against the wall and my hips to jut forward as I scooted up the wall. Holding me wide open with his body, he stabbed his cock into my cunt, deep, and kept stabbing. Hard. Filling all of me. Stretching me. Again and again. The veins in his neck and arms straining at the effort.

My flesh was tight and unprepared, and his was big and rigid. After he'd found his way in, it didn't hurt, really, not physically anyway. But sex with no eye contact, no caressing, no kissing, no connection at the soul level was just raw fucking. And while pure, out-of-control, rutting sex had its merits, and its moments, this felt empty and unsatisfying. To me. But not to Nick. This act was about an animalistic need to dominate, to punish, to own, to take, to forget, like his life depended on winning whatever battle had set him on this forceful course.

Nick fucked me against that wall, harder and faster, grunting in a steady, rapid beat with every stroke, his hips slapping furiously against my thighs. Almost instantly, his lips pulled back over his clenched teeth, his eyes squeezed tight, his face contorted, and he came with a loud, long, rough growl that originated from a deep, dark place inside him. The heat and power of his release consumed me from the inside out. One final thrust and it was done, his cock spasming inside me.

In the aftermath, the roar that had surrounded us dissipated until it was quiet.

His head dropped against the wall by mine.

His labored breathing rasped in my ear.

His heart punching against my chest squeezed my lungs.

His slaked lust, musky and hot, swirled inside me.

Although his arms and cock and body were holding me up, my legs were shaking, my stomach clenching. He was shaking too, like the joining had stripped him of his strength.

He released one of my legs and then the other, slowly, until my feet touched the floor. His spent cock slid from my pussy but he kept it pressed against me and just stood there, his palms flat on the wall, trying to still the emotions racing through his body.

It took him twice as long to still as he had to come. But soon he did. And when he did, he curled his hands around my shoulders, his fingers biting into my skin, and pulled me against his chest, wrapping his arms like chains around my waist and back, holding me tight to him, clinging to me, not in possession but in what felt like fear.

"Angel, I'm sorry," he whispered, his voice jagged but sincere. "I'm sorry."

I didn't speak. I didn't raise my hands to touch him. I didn't look at him. I just stood there, letting him hold me, and trying to make sense of what had happened and decide what I wanted to do about it.

He picked me up in his arms and walked down the hall to his bedroom, laid me on one of the twin beds and, after disposing of the condom and fastening his jeans, curled around me.

"I don't just want sex," he whispered, his cinnamon breath teasing my face, his soft gaze capturing mine. "I want you. I fucking love you, Angel. But there are things I can't talk about. Not yet. Forgive me for hurting you, and for being an asshole. I won't do that again."

Listening to his heartfelt apology made me feel like the asshole. I had made it clear that we couldn't be more than just sex—no dates, no outward signs of friendship—and yet he was apologizing to me for doing it. Why should he treat me like anything but the fuck buddies we were? Why should he treat me special? Why should he be an open book to me? Why would I expect that?

I shouldn't expect it, but I did. I didn't deserve it, but I wanted it. Despite my insistence that we maintain a secret, sex-only relationship, I wanted to be special to him. I wanted us to be close. I wanted to know him. I didn't just want sex from him either. I wanted more.

If he hadn't apologized, talked to me, explained his actions, I might have walked out the door and never seen him again. But even the little he did tell me made me feel like, with time and patience and love, we could be closer. We could be more.

My hand rose to his face and caressed it. I kissed his mouth. "I'll forgive you. If you'll forgive me for pushing you. I want to know you, so I'm going to ask questions. But I won't push further than you're willing to go. You don't need to hurt me, or insult me, or push me away to keep me from getting too close. You just need to say something. Okay?"

He nodded.

"You forgive me?" I asked.

"Yes. You forgive me?" he asked as I kissed his forehead.

"Of course."

His mouth went to mine, and he kissed me. Softly,

gently, lovingly, showing me his love. Then he moved down, between my legs, and with his mouth and his tongue and his hands caressed and loved my pussy. With licks and kisses and gentle thrusts inside me, he soothed the sore flesh he'd battered, and soon I was spiraling out of the galaxy on the orgasm he'd created just for me.

"If we didn't have to leave in one minute, I'd make love to you right," he said afterward as he held me, kissed me, caressed me, loved me, connected to me.

"And I'd let you. I only came once, and I'm not pleased." I teased him, wanting to lift the mood between us.

"That's all *I* got," he said with a grin.

"Yeah, but I'm used to getting two or three."

He chuckled. "You're a spoiled brat, you know that?"

"You're right, I am. But you're the one who spoiled me, as far as orgasms go."

Laughing, he left my arms and stood, pulled me up and into his arms. "I love it when you say that."

"Say what?"

"You're right."

"I'll always tell you when you're right. And when you're not." I put my arms around his neck. "You need to tell me too."

"I will if you're ever right."

"Jerk!" I said with a chuckle, and bit his lip.

He laughed. I loved to hear him laugh. Loved knowing I could make him laugh.

"I'm kidding," he said, staring into my eyes. "Baby, you're always right." He kissed me again, and I felt his love.

Taking my hand, he led me to the living room. He picked up the condom wrapper and stuffed it into his pocket. Scooping up my panties, he went to his knees and slid the silky material up my legs and into place, then dropped a sweet kiss on my mound.

****

We raced back to school. Nick and I shared a piece of gum and a final kiss, then he left the car, heading toward the English building, and I left the car after him, heading toward the history building. My teacher gave me a nasty look of warning and a head shake as I walked in four minutes late and slid into the seat next to Gena. It was then that I remembered I'd forgotten to warn Nick about Tyler.

Ten minutes later, a girl I recognized only as a freshman came to the door and gave my teacher a note.

"Angela, you're to report to Mr. Wilson's office," she said. "Take your things."

I got the usual you're-in-trouble noise from the class, and I shot Gena a questioning look as I grabbed my backpack. I'd never been called to the office before.

When I arrived, Mr. Wilson's secretary, Mrs. Messier, greeted me with a venomous stare and pointed at the row of chairs lining the wall in front of Mr. Wilson's office.

I looked at them, then back at her. "Why was I called here?"

"Take a seat, please."

She'd said please, but the pinhole mouth the word had to pass through squeezed any sweetness from its meaning. In defiance, I stood against the wall with my arms crossed. I heard her sigh in irritation. For some reason, knowing I'd caused it made me smile.

She picked up the handset on her desk phone and jabbed a couple of buttons with her bony finger. "Ms. Abbott is here."

A minute or two later, the door opened and Mr. Wilson called me in. My gaze flew to the chairs in front of his desk where the only two guys I'd ever slept with now sat. Both looked pissed, like they wanted to kill each other.

Chapter Six

Mr. Wilson pulled up a chair for me between Nick and Tyler. "Have a seat, Ms. Abbott."

When I was seated, he perched one leg on his desk and leaned toward me. "You left campus at lunch time today."

"Well, yeah. We talked. About Ming."

He held up his hand and smiled. "Yes, yes, but before you and I talked or afterward, before you actually pulled out of the parking lot, did you see anyone else in the lot?"

My eyes flickered, desperately wanting to turn toward Nick, to maybe get the appropriate answer from him, but I kept them straight ahead, on Wilson's face. I paused, not wanting to answer any questions until I knew what he was really asking.

"Now, this is important, so think about it carefully before you answer."

"Yeah, Angela. Think hard." Tyler's comment made me want to slap him, but instead I shot him a dirty look.

"Mr. Carrington, I told you to keep quiet." Wilson snapped at Tyler, who slunk deeper into his chair. His cast was off, and he had no trouble jiggling his leg, a habit I knew to mean he was barely containing his anger.

I took a chance. "No, Mr. Wilson."

Tyler came up out of his seat. "Just because she didn't see him doesn't mean he didn't break my windows."

"If I have to tell you one more time to keep your rear in the chair and your mouth shut, I'll put you in detention. Is that clear?" Wilson stared him back down into his seat.

Tyler scrunched his mouth up tighter than an asshole.

"Thank you, Ms. Abbott," Wilson said. "Go on back to class."

"I know he did it," Tyler insisted. "And if no one can corroborate his lame story that he left school for lunch at that time then you're obligated to file a report with the police so this asshole can pay to fix my car."

"This is bullshit," Nick mumbled.

"Mr. Spencer, is there anyone who saw you at lunch, anyone who could vouch for you? A neighbor who saw you enter your house and can give us a time? The person you left with? Your motorcycle was in the school lot the entire time, so if you left campus, you had to have ridden with someone."

This time my gaze did go to Nick, but his eyes wouldn't meet mine. His face was red from anger, from the injustice of the accusation, from the realization that the only one who could speak for him wouldn't, to protect her own reputation. He clenched his jaw and shook his head.

He was keeping quiet for me.

Tyler grunted and stood. "You take care of this, Wilson, or I'll have my father in here to do it." He shot Nick a triumphant look and left, leaving the door wide open.

Mr. Wilson sighed and moved around his desk to sit in his chair. "Ms. Abbott, you can leave now."

I felt glued to the chair. I didn't want to leave Nick in this situation. But what choice did I have? I slowly stood, turned, and walked to the door. I thought I heard a little sound come from Nick—I imagined it was the sound of his heart breaking, but I wasn't sure. My own heart was beating so hard, the only thing I could really hear clearly was it telling me what I'd known all along that I had to do.

I shut the door, walked back to Mr. Wilson's desk, and sat back in the chair next to Nick. Both his head and Wilson's snapped up, and two sets of eyes filled with questions looked at me.

"Angela, I said you could leave."

"Mr. Wilson, Nick didn't damage Tyler's car."

"How do you know that?"

I looked into Nick's eyes, smiled at him, and took his hand in mine.

"Because he and I were together at the time it supposedly happened."

The light dazzling in Nick's eyes when I told the truth for him made my heart rise in joy. After what happened today at his house, I felt like I had earned a little more of his trust. A little more of his love. Simply by doing what was right. By being brave enough to stand up for him. It felt awesome.

"He wasn't with you when I saw you."

"He was with me before that, right after class when lunch started. We were making plans to leave campus during lunch. He went to get his backpack from his locker, and I went to my car. He came right from the commons to my car. I picked him up just after you left

98

me. If he had done it, I'd have seen him. I'd have heard Tyler's alarm. Nick didn't do it. He wouldn't do it."

"Are you sure, Angela? This isn't some kind of story he's convinced you to tell to save him from trouble?"

Rage at the accusation ripped away the kindness he had admired in me earlier.

"After you left me, I saw Nick walking toward the parking lot to join me. You stopped him, asked to see his class schedule because you didn't believe him when he told you he had lunch. He dug his schedule out of his backpack, showed it to you, and you threw it back at him and stormed away, mad because you didn't catch him doing something that you could bust him for."

Nick's hand squeezed mine as if saying my words and tone were tiptoeing the line of getting us both into big trouble. I saw how close I was when I noticed Mr. Wilson's face pale and his mouth thin to the width of a toothpick.

"He and I left campus right after that," I continued, with a calmer, more respectful tone. "No alarms were going off. We didn't get back until a couple of minutes after class started. I left my car after he did. I saw him go into his building. He wasn't on campus when it happened. He didn't do it. He's not that kind of person."

Nick stood and so did I. I grabbed my backpack.

"I take it I'm in the clear now?" he asked Wilson and slipped his arm around me. I left it there. It felt so good. So right.

Mr. Wilson stood too. "Yes," he said, the word snapping off his tongue. He pointed at Nick. "But the next time you two are late to class after having lunch

99

together off campus, I'll throw you both in detention and call your parents to discuss whether this is the right school for you."

He stormed to the door, opened it, and stood by like a sentinel. Before we crossed the doorway, Mr. Wilson stuck out his arm to halt Nick.

"I'm watching you." He whispered the warning through his teeth, but I heard it clearly. The threat behind it.

Nick smiled and continued out the door. I followed, my hand in his, but Wilson stopped me with a hand on my arm.

"I'd like a word with you before you return to class."

I took a last look at Nick before the closing door severed our gaze.

"Ms. Abbott—Angela—in the four years you've been in this school, you've never caused a bit of trouble. You earn stellar grades and get along with everyone, students and faculty alike. You're from an upstanding family with high standards and aspirations. What are you doing with Spencer?"

The truth that sprang to mind—having great sex—brought a smile to my face. "Do you really want me to answer that?"

Mr. Wilson's face reddened. "I know your parents; they wouldn't be pleased with your choice."

"It's my choice."

"He's the wrong kind of boy for you."

"Who's the right kind for me? Tyler? An arrogant, mean jerk who drinks too much and hits me? Is that what I deserve?"

"Well, no, I—"

I softened my tone. "Nick is decent and kind and thoughtful of my feelings. He makes me feel safe and warm and good. He'd never hurt me, physically or emotionally. I do have standards; that's how I know I deserve someone good like Nick."

Mr. Wilson averted his eyes as if my heartfelt honesty was just too much to take.

"I don't know what happened to form your low opinion of him—I hate to think it's just the size of his family's bank account—but he's not what you think. If there's anyone you should be keeping an eye on, it's not Nick Spencer." I opened the door. "It's his accuser."

He grabbed the door to stop me. "Let me warn you, Ms. Abbott, you don't know your boyfriend as well as you think you do. Be careful."

He released the door, and after I left it shut on the questions that tumbled in my brain.

The bell rang as I left Wilson's office, so I raced to the commons to see if I could catch Nick before he left for work. He wasn't there and, when I reached the parking lot, I saw his motorcycle speeding away. It was Friday, which meant I wouldn't see him until Monday.

Unless I went to his house. Or he came to mine. But of course, that wouldn't happen.

****

My parents invited Tyler and his parents to our house for dinner on Saturday. As much as I begged to be let out of it, my parents held firm—I would attend.

"I swear, Betsi, one of these days I'm going to lure Carmen away from you. She's the best cook in town." Rhonda Carrington, Tyler's mother, patted her flat stomach and settled with a sigh onto one of the white

Spanish leather couches in our formal living room.

"Glad you enjoyed the meal." My mother shot a satisfied little smile at my dad as she sat next to him. He gave her an equally proud smile with his eyes as he laid his arm along her shoulders.

"I swear we'd pay that woman whatever she asked," Rhonda continued. "Wouldn't we, Rey?"

Reynold Carrington, Tyler's father, stood at the bar mixing himself his usual. He snorted. "We would have until someone vandalized Tyler's car. Now we're in no position to lure away a top-notch chef."

"Oh, no," Mom cried, turning to Tyler. "Not your new sports car?"

Tyler nodded pathetically, looking like he'd lost his best friend. "He broke all the windows."

"He? You know who's responsible?" my dad asked.

"I know who did it," Tyler said, his eyes darting to me.

"Good," Mom added. "At least you won't have to pay for the damages yourself."

Rey sipped his drink and went to sit by his wife. "Tyler knows who did it, but apparently the boy has an alibi, so Wilson won't pursue it."

The conversation and the lies were turning my stomach. I got up from the love seat and headed to the kitchen for a bottle of sparkling water to calm my queasiness. Then I'd sneak up the back stairway to my room. As if she knew my plan, Mom grabbed my hand as I went by and pulled me next to her on the couch. I glowered at her, but she glowered right back and held my hand captive, knowing I'd bolt otherwise. She was right.

"That hardly seems fair considering Tyler is so certain," Mom said. "Who was it? No one we know, I hope?"

"Nick Spencer." Tyler practically spat out the name.

"Spencer?" Dad asked, his eyes flying to me. "Isn't that the boy who gave you a ride home a month or so ago?"

I felt everyone's eyes burning into me, and Mom's hand had a death grip on mine, but I couldn't sit still or keep quiet another minute.

I jumped to my feet. "He didn't do it."

Tyler jumped up too, facing me. "How do you know?" he accused. "You told Wilson you didn't even see him that day."

"I know he has an alibi that proves he wasn't even at school when it happened."

"I'm sure his 'witness' lied to protect him," he cut back.

"Why do you hate him so much? Why do you want to mess up his life?"

"Why do you care so much?"

"Because I—"

In the silence that followed my halted response, I realized I was two blinks from outing my relationship with Nick...something I wasn't ready to do. I corralled my temper and fought to keep the emotion from my voice.

"Because I think it's wrong to blame him for something he didn't do. Why do you care so little about that?"

Before Tyler could respond, Rey spoke up. "Are you friends with this boy, Angela?"

"Not really. I mean, I know him." Technically I wasn't lying. Nick and I were much more than friends. And in the biblical sense, I did know him. Very well.

"You might want to stay away from him," he warned.

"You know something about him?" Mom asked Rey.

He sipped his drink. "When Tyler told me about this Spencer character, I did some checking. The full report hasn't come in yet, but what has trickled in does not make for a pretty picture. He was expelled from several schools for fighting, truancy, vandalism, and various inappropriate and lewd activities. When he was thirteen, he had a brush with the law for drunken and disorderly conduct, but he was a minor and it was his first real offense so the judge gave him probation. The offense isn't on his record, but the judge is a friend of mine, who remembered the case well."

I swallowed the bitterness in my throat as Mom asked the question I wanted to ask. "Any recent problems?"

Rey shook his head. "Doesn't seem to be. But he lives in a seedy neighborhood—drugs, high crime rate, gang activity. Once a hot-headed boy gets a taste of trouble…"

Would these people think any differently if they knew the trouble started right after Nick's dad deserted the family? The truth gnawed at me, clawed to get out. I wanted to slap them with *that* truth, but how could I explain why I knew such intimate details about a guy I claimed not to be friends with? And for some reason, I felt the need to protect Nick's secrets from them, knowing they wouldn't understand and would just use the information against him. But I could say something in his defense.

"Living in a bad neighborhood doesn't make a person bad any more than living in a good one makes a person good," I said. "A lot of people turn their lives around after a false step. Remember Darren Mathews down the street? He was cooking meth in the family's guest house, selling it. He served his time and now speaks out against drugs in high schools around the country. If Nick hasn't had any trouble for a while, it's clear that the earlier stuff was just, you know, a little stumble, not a way of living."

"Damn, Angela, it's pretty sad that you're so quick to defend a guy like him but not me, your boyfriend." Tyler jumped in.

"We broke up, remember?"

"What?" Rhonda exclaimed from the couch, her voice distressed. "When did this happen?"

Rey put his arm around his wife's shoulders to prevent her from getting too excited. Rhonda was always on some kind of mood-altering substance, either to calm her down or rev her up.

"I'm sure it's just a little lover's spat, Ronnie," he said, keeping his tone calm and light and giving Tyler the eye. "Tyler, you and Angela need to work out this little squabble of yours on your own." He stood, reached into his pocket for his car keys, and tossed them to Tyler. "Get out of here. Go for a drive. Kiss and make up."

Everyone laughed at the "kiss and make up" part. Everyone but me.

"And don't come back until you do," Rhonda added and grabbed the drink from her husband's hand

105

and downed the two fingers of amber liquor chilling at the bottom of the highball like it was apple juice instead of a fifty-year-old single malt whiskey.

"I'd rather have my toenails pulled out. Excuse me." I turned away with the intent to dash up the stairs to my room, but Dad caught my arm at the elbow, the frown on his face so hard it could cut cement.

"Excuse *me*, young lady, but you will not be rude to these people who are like family to you. You will apologize, and you will go with Tyler to work things out between you."

The only way out of this one was to tell them everything, including the truth about Nick and me. I looked at my parents, anger, disappointment, and embarrassment weighing heavy on their faces and bodies. I wasn't ready for the disaster that would hit if I told them the truth and the pain it would cause them. And me.

I turned toward the Carringtons. Rhonda's blue eyes were vacant but soft and kind, her mouth curved in a small, loving smile. She had bought me my first bra when my mom couldn't face the reality that those really were breasts filling out my T-shirts.

When my dad was neck-deep in an important trial and never home, it had been Rey who had taught me to waltz in preparation for my first cotillion. He looked at me now with patience and humor in his gray eyes.

They had been a part of our every family holiday celebration, large and small, since before I was born. There was a time I'd spent more time at their house than my own. I might not share all their beliefs, but they'd always loved me like their own. That knowledge softened my heart and tempered my anger.

"I apologize for my rudeness."

The thick carpet muffled the sound of my heels as I crossed the room to them and hugged them sincerely. They hugged me back like all was immediately forgotten and forgiven.

"Ty, take Angela for some ice cream." Dad pulled a twenty from his wallet and handed it to him. "Chocolate always cheers her up. And bring a quart back for the ladies."

I didn't want to go, but I also didn't want to create another scene. The adults stared at Tyler and me, pushing us out the door with their eyes. Right before I climbed into Rey's car, I saw the four of them head outside to the patio. Dad had been eager to show off the new grill he'd rarely use.

As we drove, memories of the last time I was in the car with Tyler rose up and lodged in my throat. If I tried to eat ice cream now, it wouldn't go down.

"I miss you," Tyler said.

I didn't respond.

"Look, I know my drinking bugs you, so I've stopped."

I didn't believe him for a second. "Good for you."

"Baby, we've been together for a long time. Give us another chance. Give me another chance."

"I'm glad you're not drinking, but I meant it when I said we're through. We can be civil to each other because of our parents, but we will never be together again."

He gripped the wheel tighter as he took a corner going twenty over the speed limit. "Are you seeing somebody?"

"Why would you think that?"

"We've broken up before, and you've always come back to me in a few days, horny as hell. We broke up almost two months ago, and you haven't come back. So maybe you're getting it from someone else."

"Have you seen me with anyone?" I held my breath on his answer. If he had seen me with Nick, it would explain why he hated him so much and wanted to cause trouble for him.

"No. But you could be sneaking around with some guy behind my back."

"You really think I'm that kind of girl?"

"No. Sorry."

I released my breath. "You and I were together because our parents wanted us together. We're not right for each other. I finally realized it. I think you did too, which is why you drank all the time."

"You're wrong. We have the same background. We want the same things. We're perfect for each other." He grabbed my hand.

I eased my hand from his and stared out the window, seeing in the passing landscape the face of the man who *was* perfect for me. And he didn't come with a silver spoon in his mouth.

Ah, Nick. I can smell you, taste you, feel your rough hands on me. All I want to do is get lost in you while you whisper all your dirty little secrets into my skin. I need to see you. Now. I'm crawling out of my skin from wanting to get to you. Can you hear my voice in your head? Come to me. Tonight. Climb through my window and into my bed. Wake me with your lips on mine, your tongue on my breasts, your hand between my legs. Please. Please.

"Please?"

Hearing my silent word said aloud pulled me from my erotic thoughts. I turned dazed eyes toward Tyler. His eyes were on me, not on the road ahead of him. His hands weren't on the wheel, they were on his knees. The car was no longer moving, but parked. I looked out the front window. The ice cream shop stood in front of us, a colorful neon sign announcing the number of flavors they offered.

"What?" I asked.

"I said, please think about it."

"Think about what?"

"About getting back together with me."

The crude URGH! noise that filled my head roughly translated to *Are you stupid? How much fucking clearer can I be?* But I didn't articulate it because I wasn't yet at the point where my only option was to crush his feelings.

"We can be friends, but that's all," I said and climbed out of the car before he could say more.

Sprinting ahead of him into the ice cream shop. I paid for my scoop of chocolate with a five I had in my pocket. I walked out of the shop while he was still ordering his and the carton to go.

The sound of a rumbling motorcycle engine caught my attention. The noisy bike was inside one of the bays at a repair shop across the street. The dark hair and broad shoulders of the mechanic in greasy coveralls working on the bike looked familiar. He stood to grab something from a shelf, and his long legs and tight ass stirred even more familiarity. Could it be I wanted to see Nick so badly I was making him materialize before me?

I walked to the edge of the street and stared into

that bay, willing the man to turn toward me. As if he'd heard my plea, his head lifted, turned left and right. Then he turned my way. And my heart fluttered.

It *was* Nick.

He stared. I stared. A grin on his face, he started forward as if he were going to cross the street to me. He stopped at the same time I felt Tyler's arm slide around my shoulder. I broke the embrace immediately, but when I looked back across the street, Nick had turned his back to me and was headed toward the shop office.

I wanted to run to him, explain what he saw. Make him understand that I wasn't with Tyler, no matter how it looked. And I had to do it now.

I should have done it. But I didn't. Because Tyler was there. He was convinced I was seeing someone. If he knew that person was Nick, he'd hurt him.

"What are you looking at?" Tyler asked, his eyes going to the shop across the street. Nick had already gone into the office, so Tyler hadn't seen him.

I stood there, staring at the empty spot where Nick had been, my heart melting in my chest like the ice cream melting down my hand from the hurt I was causing Nick and myself. I threw the chocolate mess into the trash and got into the car.

Tyler didn't say a word on the drive home. When we arrived, I ran to my room and locked the door behind me. Let him deal with the parents and the ice cream and the questions. I had bigger problems.

Dirty Little Secret

Chapter Seven

Nick was pissed. I knew by the way he avoided looking my way that next Monday, which was hard to do since we stood six lockers apart. A red flag waved on the one cheek I could see, and his jaw worked, as if grinding me between his teeth, the books he threw into his locker suffering for my sins.

Everything inside me wanted to rush over to him, press my body against his back, throw my arms around his waist, assure him what he saw meant nothing, and kiss him until he believed me.

Instead, I let him walk away without saying a word. I felt the pain of a billion wasp stings in my stomach as I watched him shove through the door like he couldn't wait to be away from me.

"Keep staring at him like that, and everybody's going to know you're crushing on him."

I turned to see Gena standing behind me, a grin on her face.

"What are you talking about?" I slammed my locker door and walked away.

She caught up with me at Nick's locker and grabbed my arm. "You know exactly what—and who—I'm talking about." She'd nodded toward his locker when she'd said "who."

"Gena, no offense, but I'm in a really lousy mood right now and, I swear, if you don't back off about him,

111

I'm going to say something we'll both regret."

She jerked back as if I'd slapped her and narrowed her eyes at me. "Let me know when the bitch leaves and my friend gets back."

An apology pried open my mouth but didn't make it past my lips until she'd already gone. I stepped closer to Nick's locker, touched it like I wanted to touch him, leaned my head against it like I wanted to lean into him, breathed in like I wanted to breathe him in. It didn't make me feel better. Only he could do that. I pushed away and headed to class.

"Ms. Abbott, a moment please."

I rolled my eyes at and silently cursed the voice calling from behind me. *Shit!* This day just kept getting better. I turned. "Can this wait, Mr. Wilson? I have class now."

"I'm pleased to hear you're actually going to class today."

I wanted to ask him if he had a point, but I thought that would get me into more trouble than I seemed to be in, so instead I bit my tongue and waited for him to continue.

"Your attendance record just came to my attention. Over the past month, you've missed class once or twice a week. Mostly the class following your lunch period."

He paused, probably to allow me to explain. I didn't.

"Would you care to explain?"

No, not really. "Time got away from me, I guess."

"I suggest you invest in a watch and get back to school in time for class, or I'll be forced to help you be on time by revoking your off-campus privileges."

"I'll work harder to be on time."

"And while you're watching the time, you might remind Mr. Spencer that his margins are even thinner."

I swallowed back the tears I felt gathering in my eyes and nodded, even though I wasn't sure what he meant by thin margins, and even though Nick would probably never speak to me again.

Wilson paused again, stared at me like he wanted to add more to his warning. My face grew hot from the creepy way his eyes stared into me. Not creepy like he was in to me, but creepy like how worried he was for me. Like he'd noticed the impending tears.

"May I go now?" I asked softly.

"Yes, go on." He immediately left my side and rushed toward the administration building. Rush seemed to be his only speed, like a wind-up toy that had been wound too tight.

After he disappeared into the building, I was alone. In another minute, I'd officially be late. Everyone else was already in class. It was just me. The silence felt thick and eerie.

I trudged toward class, feeling empty and sorry for myself. It had been three days—forever—since I'd lain in Nick's arms, felt him inside me. And now that he'd seen me with Tyler, I'd probably be waiting a lot longer. If only I could see him, talk to him, I could make him understand. I know I—

The thought had barely materialized when Nick came out of the English building, backpack slung over one wide shoulder, head down. I stopped. Stared. Willed him to look at me. As if he'd heard me, his gaze moved up, found mine, then skittered away as he passed me, as if I no longer existed to him.

Pockets of pain exploded inside me at the brush

off, sending emotional shrapnel into my heart and lungs and stomach. Was this how he felt all the times I'd ignored him in the halls, at our lockers, across campus? I couldn't breathe from the hurt.

"Nick." The sound, as rough and dry as the winter leaves racing across the cement, barely counted as a word, but it snagged his attention.

He stopped, turned to face me, his eyes boring into mine accusingly, but he didn't speak and he didn't make a move toward me. He was stone.

If we were to be fixed, all the connecting, the apologizing, the pleading would have to come from me. I walked over to him.

Now that I had his attention, I didn't know what to do with it. I went with simple.

"Hi."

A raised eyebrow was his only response. Poor guy was probably too shocked that I'd openly speak to him at school to do anything else. Taking that tiny response as a welcome sign, I stepped closer, flattening my palms on his chest like I'd done on his locker and dropped my forehead to my hands. He smelled really good, like rain and soap. I wanted to curl up next to him and bury my nose in his skin.

"Can we go somewhere and talk," I said, meeting his eyes.

"We are talking."

Wow. A whole sentence. I slid my fingers down his arms. They were warm, muscular, and I wanted them around me. "I want to do more than talk."

His pulse jumped at the base of his throat, his tongue snaked out to wet his lips. Yeah, he knew what I meant. He knew what I wanted. He swallowed, and I could see him trying to gather words. I looked into his eyes, eager to see the "yes," desperate to hear the "yes" leave his mouth. Instead I got a rude half grunt, half snort sound, followed by, "Not happening."

The "no" stunned like a punch to the chest, shifting me back half a step. Before I could react, he spun on his heel and continued on toward his bike.

"Nick." I caught up with him. He didn't respond, just kept walking with long strides I found difficult to match.

"Nick, wait." I grabbed his arm.

He stopped, yanked away from my touch. "What do you want, Angela?"

The anger flashing in his eyes and in his tone surprised me, hurt me. Those damn tears were still there, and they were weakening my ability to speak rationally. *Dammit!*

I swallowed. "You."

Though pitiful and small, the word made an impression. His eyes opened wide for a split second then lowered half way. Then he shook his head as if he didn't believe me or was disgusted by me, maybe both.

"You don't want me." He took a step closer, touched my face, and brushed away a tear rolling down my face. "Not really."

I grabbed his hand, pressing a kiss into his palm. "Yes, I do. I want you, Nick. I need you."

Joy burst inside me, telling me that it was the truth, and I felt a charge pass between us, the same charge that always sparked to life whenever we were together. He wanted me too. I heard it in his pulse at his neck. Saw it in his gaze. Felt it in his breath on my cheek.

"Ask your boyfriend to take care of your needs,"

he said angrily, and made a motion to leave.

"You are my boyfriend." Something exploded inside of me at the admission. At that moment, I knew I wanted Nick in my life for real, not just for the sex. In the short time we'd been together, I'd discovered that without him my life was only half full.

The knowledge that I'd hurt him hurt worse than any pain I'd experienced. So did the thought that I couldn't talk to him, laugh with him, touch him, be with him every day. He was a part of me now. A part I couldn't give up. We would find a way to make us work. I didn't know how. I only knew we had to try.

Unwilling to be separate from him any longer, I lunged against him, pulled his face to mine, and kissed him. For the first time, I wasn't thinking about whether anyone from school saw me. I was only thinking about making sure he understood what he meant to me.

At first he remained stone cold, but soon his lips warmed and moved against mine, his arms went around me, one hand in my hair, and his body molded into my curves. Having him attached to me again pushed out the sadness and loneliness that had filled me for days and replaced it with happiness. My soul strummed with satisfaction.

He broke off the kiss. "Are you back with Tyler?"

"No, baby." I shook my head. "Never."

"His arm around you on your ice cream date said something else."

"It's a long story, but our parents found out we broke up, so they forced us to go get ice cream to 'work out our issues.' I don't know why he put his arm around me. I mean, I had just told him again that we were done. And if you'd stayed to watch what happened next, you'd have seen me immediately move away from him, throw my ice cream into the trash, and storm off to the car."

A grin twitched on his lips. "You threw away your ice cream?"

I shrugged. "Too upset."

"Chocolate?"

I nodded, happy he remembered my lie about chocolate being my one vice.

"You really were upset."

"I was."

"What about when you got home? Did you sit on his lap and kiss him in front of mommy and daddy and act like ice cream had magically resolved everything?"

I snorted at the ridiculous thought. "I locked myself in my room."

"Ah. The spoiled-child-throwing-a-fit tactic…bet you're good at it," he teased.

"I've had some practice," I said, and playfully twisted his nipple. "Jerk."

He flinched back, making a big show of wincing in pain. "Damn, woman, I think you twisted it off."

I laughed. "Poor baby. Tell you what…" My arms slipped around his waist. "…take me somewhere, right now, and I'll give you some really fine first aid for that nipple."

"Guess I'd better do what you say. No telling what body part you'll twist off next."

"Good idea."

****

His house key was in the lock, but it wasn't turning.

"If you don't hurry up, I'm going to fuck you right

here on the porch," I growled the words into his neck and squeezed his ass. "Or on your front lawn. And I think your neighbor is watching us from her window. You'll have to explain it to your mom."

"Fuck," he growled in frustration and slammed his fists on the door. "Move back," he said. "I'm going to kick this fucking door down."

I giggled. "Move aside." I shoved him aside, pulled out the key, fitted it in again, grabbed the door handle and pulled it toward me, turning the key. The lock fought me but soon unclenched, and I opened the door. I handed him his keys, a big know-it-all smile on my face.

"Get in here." He pulled me into the house.

The door had barely slammed shut behind us before we were down the hall and in his room. His mouth was on mine at the same time his arms wound around me. His hands splayed across my ass and pressed me closer to the hardness held in by his zipper.

The fire that had burned low in my stomach since we'd left school flared to high, consuming everything until only desire controlled my body. I ground my pelvis into his, showing him how much I wanted him. I grabbed the hem of his T-shirt, pulled it up his chest and over his head, and let it drop to the floor.

My mouth brushed over his injured nipple teasingly, lovingly, then the other one. My jealous tongue joined in the fun, licking the tiny puckered nibs until Nick groaned in pleasure.

"That's some pretty fine first aid."

"There's more."

My mouth wandered downward, across the valleys and peaks of his ribs, over his tight, muscled stomach, around his belly-button, to the waistband of his jeans guarding the treasures below. I moved back up over familiar territory to his mouth. I kissed him, stroking his tongue with mine, while my hands moved to his pants. I attacked the stud, prying it from its tight slit, and tugging the zipper down.

Wanting all of him, I pushed his jeans and boxers down over his hips, and with both hands held his cock, stroking him, tugging him. He toed off his boots and stepped on the hem of his jeans to get them down his legs and off. He cupped my face in his large hands, brushed his thumb against my jaw. I looked into his face. His eyes were alight with love and passion, and I hoped he could see the same emotions in mine.

"I want you, Nick. I need you. Just you. Never doubt that."

"I hope so."

I would show him, change "hope" to "know." Unable to wait any longer to feel his hands on my skin, I yanked off my shirt and undid my bra, tossing them to the floor. My breasts spilled out, full and heavy, my nipples hard and ready for his mouth. He palmed them, squeezing them together, and dropped his head to fit them into his mouth, first one, then the other.

My hands lowered to my skirt, unbuttoned and unzipped it, and it fell. His mouth and hands left my breasts long enough to yank my panties down my legs. Then his mouth was on mine, his hand between my legs. I was so ready for him, for his touch, that he was able to easily slide one long finger inside me. At the rush of it, I held his cock tighter in my hands, stroking it, pinching the wet head, caressing his tight balls.

The feeling of him beating in my hands, of his

fingers inside me, melted the bones in my body, but I managed to raise one leg and wrap it around his hip, giving him all the room he needed.

As his finger plunged in and out of my hole, his palm pressed against my clit, rubbing it into a frenzy of white-hot desire. We would burn up if we didn't extinguish this inferno soon.

I broke away from his consuming kiss and embrace and pushed him back onto the bed. "Spread your legs," I demanded.

Grinning, he did as I asked.

I lay between his legs, my mouth going to his cock. I licked the head, circling my tongue on it, lapping the pre-cum gathered at the slit. He put his hands on my head, gathered my hair in his fingers, back from my face, so he could watch me devour him. I licked down the shaft, and sucked his balls one at a time into my mouth.

A groan rumbled in his chest, and his legs widened a little more as his hips flexed in appreciation. I looked up into his face. His eyes were half closed, his lips parted, and a look of bliss covered his face. I loved to make him feel good. I'd do anything to put that look on his face.

I drew his fully rigid dick into my mouth, sucking as I worked up and down it, my lips tightening around his swelled flesh, my tongue sliding along it.

"Angel...Ahh fuck. It's fucking fantastic, but I don't want to come yet." His hand in my hair stopped me. "I want to eat you."

"Okay, but I want to come with you inside me. Promise me you'll stop when I say stop."

"I promise."

I lay back and let my legs fell open to his mouth. To his talented, talented mouth.

He dove into my muff, kissing my swollen pussy lips, nibbling them, sucking them, letting his lips taste it all. I let my legs go up and wider, and his tongue thoroughly licked my wet cleft before zipping across the swollen clit, then back into my core, over and over, his mouth ravaging me like he was starved for my taste. The sight of his mouth on me, his head there at my most tender place, bringing me pleasure, jacked up the pressure inside my core.

His mouth left me, and my eyes shot to him in distress. He was looking up at me, his lips parted. As he watched me, he plunged one finger into my hole, fucked me. I circled my hips against that digit, thrust up, taking it deeper inside me, and moaned.

"Come for me, Angel," he said, his low voice rough, demanding. "Come in my mouth."

I nodded wobbly, and his head went back to my pussy. He flicked his tongue over my clit as his finger stroked my tunnel, and I couldn't stop it, didn't want to stop it, didn't want to say the word that would stop it. I cried out, coming against his mouth.

My hands gripping his hair, he stroked me faster, lapped my juices like a man starved. When I calmed, he rose up on his knees, a pleased grin on his wet face, his eyes shining with need. He reached under his mattress and pulled out a condom, tore it open, and rolled it down his long, thick package.

"You promised," I half-heartedly complained, my hips still writhing with the pleasure coursing through me, my hands cupping my breasts, making me feel ripe all over, ready for him to plunge into me.

"You didn't say stop." He lifted me up, pulled me on his lap and leaned back so that I was on him. "Ride my cock."

My limbs were wet noodles, but I managed to straddle him. Then I was sinking down onto his erection, his cock going so deep into my pussy he'd never get out.

His eyes linked with mine, his hands linked with mine, I leaned over him, his arms straight, holding my weight. I rocked on him, leaning in so my clit rubbed along his cock as it slid in and out. This position gave me control, allowed me to feel the head of his cock as it speared me, hitting my E, F, and G-spots, rushing me fast to my climax.

I looked down to where we were joined, his flesh in mine, and heat flooded me as I watched us fuck. I was almost there again. I focused on his face, wanting it to be the last thing I saw before my vision clouded and broke apart.

His eyes were hazy on mine, his hips pressing up against mine in a contrast rhythm, and I felt his cock swell inside my wet tunnel, making my grip tighter on him.

I put my hands on his chest and leaned over a little more. His hands rubbed up and down my thighs then went around my hips and squeezed my ass cheeks, keeping me firmly impaled on his cock as I rode him.

He lifted his head and drew a nipple into his mouth, sucking it, moaning around it, the sound vibrating through me. He moved under me in a constant rhythm, working us together even tighter, and I watched his face, watched the pleasure build, knew it was coming, that he was just waiting for me to find mine first.

He shifted one hand between us to where we were connected. Two fingers found my clit and pinched it in the V a few times. It was just the spark I needed to erupt.

I bore down on his cock, my head back, and I growled his name as I came. Immediately, he rolled us over, took the top spot for himself, and pounded into me, grunting as he did. His mouth went to mine and we kissed, sucking, biting, and tongue fucking as we loved each other. I bucked up against his thrusts, our moans mixing in our mouths as he filled the condom.

He was right. Sex was my vice. No. *He* was.

****

Contentment and sexual satisfaction has a way of making a body sleepy. Sometime after filling our third condom, we fell asleep in each other's arms, nothing covering our bodies but cooling sweat and the smell of each other's pleasure.

Something, a soft sound or maybe the feeling of a presence, jolted me from my dozing. I lifted my head from Nick's shoulder for a better listen. A boy, about ten or eleven with blond hair and dark eyes, stood in the doorway, his eyes and mouth comically wide as he studied us, took in the sight of two naked bodies wrapped around each other. The soft sound that had pricked holes in my slumber had been his labored breathing.

"Nick," I whispered. "We've got company."

Nick's eyes popped open, and his gaze followed my nod toward the door. He bolted up and pulled the sheet over my naked body. "Simon, get the hell out of here."

"I'm telling Mom." Simon disappeared from the doorway and ran down the hall. We heard him talking but I couldn't make out the words. We also heard a response in a female voice.

"Shit. My mom's home?" He leaned over me to look at the alarm clock sitting on the table between the twin beds. "Oh, fuck. It's four o'clock. I'm supposed to be at work."

He jumped out of bed and shut and locked the door. He grabbed our discarded clothes from the floor and dropped them in a pile on the bed. We dressed as fast as we could. Pounding on the door sped us along even faster.

"Steven Nicholas Spencer! Open this door. Simon said you're in there with a naked girl." More pounding, followed by more shouting. "Get your butt out here right this minute, or I will break down this door."

Ah, so that's where he got it.

He grinned. "Sorry, Angel. This is going to be fucking awkward."

I grinned back, as if to say, we're in it together. "I'll get you for this, Steven Nicholas Spencer."

Laughing, he pulled on his boots, and when my shoes were on too, he pulled me into his arms.

"Ready for the firing squad?"

"No. But let's get it over with."

He kissed me good in case it would be our last, then grabbed my hand and opened the door, keeping me behind him. I half expected his mother to attack us right then and there, but she didn't. She wasn't even there. Hand in hand we walked down the hallway into the living room. His mother sat in the rocker, rocking furiously.

She was a handsome woman, with long hair the color of Nick's and dark eyes that snapped with anger and disappointment. She rose from the chair, arms crossed over her chest. Her unflattering clothes did nothing to accentuate her tall, slim figure.

Nick put his arm around me. "Mom, this is Angela. Angela, my mom, Elena."

"Mrs. Spencer, it's nice to meet you."

"First of all, I'm not a Mrs., so don't call me that. Second, I'm sure you'd agree that we're not meeting under the best circumstances, and if you won't judge me by our first meeting, I won't judge you either. Third, I have family business to discuss with my son, so I'll ask you to leave. Now."

I leaned up and kissed Nick's mouth. "See you later." I had headed toward the door, my backpack in my hand, when Nick grabbed my wrist and pulled me back against his side, his arm around me.

"Mom, I'm her ride home."

"It's okay," I whispered, and dropped my hand on his chest. "I'll walk or call someone. You need to get to work."

"No," he said to me, then turned back to his mom. "We'll talk when I get home from work," he continued. "Right now, I have to go."

That wasn't the answer his mother wanted to hear; I could see it in her face, her snapping eyes, her tight mouth, but she didn't argue.

He grabbed his jacket and his helmet and ushered me out the door ahead of him.

Outside, he pulled on the jacket and climbed on the bike to start it.

I put my backpack on, then climbed on behind him.

125

He handed me the helmet, and I put it on.

His mother's face stared out through the living room window at us as we zoomed away.

When he stopped at the end of my driveway, I got off and took off the helmet and handed it to him. Before he pulled it on, he pulled me in for a kiss, said "Love you," and left.

I didn't envy Nick the scene he'd be coming home to tonight. I couldn't help but feel a little responsible for it. I was the one who'd tempted him into going to his house to make love. Not that he took all that much convincing. I smiled, remembering how we'd loved each other today.

When I no longer saw Nick's bike on the road, I turned to go in. Despite the many differences in our two houses, there was one key feature they shared: a concerned mother staring out the living room window at her child, revealing in her frowning face all the anger and disappointment that filled her soul.

I walked in, and my mother started crying. "You can't be with that boy, Angela. You just can't."

"Mom, I'm not…" I immediately went to my go-to answer, to deny our relationship, but I couldn't do it. "Mom. I want to be with him. I *am* with him, whether anybody likes it or not. He makes me happy." Surely she could see and hear the love I had for him and would understand. But just to make sure, I added, "I love him."

My declaration only seemed to infuriate her. "I don't care what you want or what you *think* you feel," she shouted. Her anger scorched her tears, but there were too many for it to dry them all. "Your father and I will *not* let you throw away your future on that boy."

"I'm not throwing away anything. Nick's—"

"Don't you even speak his name in this house!"

I'd never seen my mother so furious with me or with anyone that she screamed at the top of her lungs. It scared me. Momentarily stole my words.

"You will break it off with him, immediately, and never, *ever,* see him again." Her voice was lower than before but still as lethal.

"Or what?" I asked in a tone that was the closest to sassing my mother I'd ever come.

Her hand whipped toward my face, her open palm connecting with my cheek. A starburst of heat exploded in my face, and pain stung the softest part of my heart. She'd slapped me. She'd never hit me before. Never spanked me. Never raised a hand to me. My hand flew to my face. Tears gathered in my eyes but for once had no effect on her.

"We can make life extremely difficult for that boy. Don't make the mistake of thinking we won't."

"You don't have the right to tell me what to do or who to love. I'm not twelve."

"I'm your mother. You live in my house. And you will do as I say."

"Why are you doing this to me?" I shouted, angry and shocked by the stranger living in my mother's body.

"Because we love you, want what's best for you, want to protect you from people who could harm you."

"I have nothing to fear from Ni—from him. I promise you. He's a good person, Mom. He gets good grades. He works after school to help take care of his mom and brother. He—"

"It's you who doesn't know him. He's a *murderer*,

Angela."

Every system in my body skipped a beat, leaving me ice cold. "What?"

She grabbed a report from the side table and stuck it out to me. "Read this. Then I dare you to debate your lover's fine characteristics with me."

I kept my hands at my side, my eyes on that report. I didn't want to read it. It would reveal secrets that would mess up what I had with Nick.

She grabbed my hand and slapped the report into it. "Read it."

I clutched it in my hand and ran upstairs to my room, slamming the door and locking it. I threw the report across the room, where it hit the wall and landed with a soft thwump onto the thick carpet. Tears burst up out of me like a fountain. I threw myself onto my bed, bawling myself to sleep.

Soft knocking at me door woke me sometime later, but I didn't respond. My room was dark, and it was dark outside my window. I wondered whether Nick had made it home already. Was he eating a silent dinner with his family, his food tasting like mush in his mouth because of the anger and hurt feelings seasoning it? Or had he and his mom talked it out, resolved some issues, adjusted the rules to fit in his new role as a grown son who has taken a lover? Or, like me, had the world he'd known been so irrevocably changed after the big explosion that it would be years before he found his place in it again?

What was it about Nick that my parents hated so much? "They don't even know him," I said, the sound of my voice strange and loud in the quiet room.

You don't know him, my mother's voice crawled

through my brain. Hadn't Mr. Wilson said something similar?

My gaze flew across the room to the floor where I'd thrown the report. I got up, grabbed it, and settled back in bed. I turned on my lamp and began to read.

Chapter Eight

Stephen Nicholas Spencer was a good student and athlete, with a good attitude and never a problem until age thirteen when his father, Collin Spencer, announced he was leaving his family—wife Elena and sons Nick and Simon—for his lover, Melissa Jenkins.

Police were summoned to the Spencer home on a domestic violence call and found the father unconscious on the floor with multiple stab wounds, mother unconscious on the floor with a concussion and contusions, and Nick covered with contusions, cuts, and blood. Nick was arrested for stabbing his father, who was hospitalized and later died. The stabbing initially was called a contributing factor to the death, but medical evidence proved the two incidences were unrelated. A weak/malfunctioning heart was the official cause of death. Mrs. Spencer testified that Nick had acted in self-defense and in the defense of his family from his father's attacks.

Jenkins pulled a gun on Mrs. Spencer at the funeral. Nick stepped in to protect his mother. He and Jenkins struggled. The gun went off. Jenkins died at the scene from a bullet to the heart. Investigation and witnesses confirmed Nick acted in self-defense and in defense of his family.

After the deaths, Nick had increasing trouble at school, in society, and with the law. He was arrested for being under the influence of an illegal substance at a school event and breaking the nose of the officer attempting to escort him out. As a minor he received probation.

He attended four different schools over a span of two years, and was suspended numerous times at each for excessive truancy, fighting on school premises, engaging in sexual activities with female classmates on school premises, attending class under the influence of drugs and/or alcohol. Expulsions followed when behaviors continued and escalated.

The family moved twice, the last time to Rockford Falls two years ago. At the request of Nick's aunt, Carla Messier, dean's secretary at Rockford Academy for nearly thirty years, he was admitted to the private college preparatory school on the condition that he cause no trouble. The school agreed to give him a chance to start over academically so he could graduate, improve his chances of getting into college, and get his life back on track. One infraction and he would be out of school and probably on a fast track to prison.

The report went on and on, listing the various infractions that comprised Nick's troubles, and wrapped up with a copy of Nick's most recent grades. All A's except for one. All of his teachers provided glowing comments about his academic performance and some concern about his solitude and lack of friends, and his English teacher commented that his excessive absences in her class would likely bring his A down to a D if he didn't get back on course. English was the class after lunch that we often missed because we were in the middle of each other. The last page included a narrative from Headmaster Wilson commenting on Nick's numerous absences in the past couple of months and on how close he was to breaking his conditions for staying on at the school.

Nick's troubles in school now were because of me, our relationship. I was as bad for him as he was for me.

Our relationship had a troubling effect on me too. I'd alienated and worried my parents. Insulted family friends who are like second parents to me. Broken it off with my long-time boyfriend. Bitched out and lied to my best friend. Ditched more class in two months than I'd done all four years of high school combined, risking my academic future. Sassed my headmaster. Made my mother angry enough to slap me for the first time in my life. Had sex with a stranger. Had fallen in love with same stranger, a guy who has a long, dark, troubled past that was foreign and scary to me and who was unlikely to ever be able to give me anything but heartache.

I risked everything I was, everything I'd ever wanted in my future, all for a chance to be with someone who made me feel, for the first time, my heart beating in my chest, someone who made me happier and more satisfied than I'd ever felt. And now I had to pay the consequences. I had to give up Nick Spencer, the man I loved. For both our futures. Before the people who loved me made things "very difficult" for him.

****

A few days later, two days before Thanksgiving break, I had made my decision.

I left Nick a note to meet me in our spot past the soccer field at lunch. When he got there, he pulled me into his arms and kissed me. The weak person I am, I folded, taking him in greedily. *Way to hang strong, Angela.*

132

"I've wanted to do that all day," he said, then picked me up and spun me around, making me squeal.

"Nick, put me down."

He lowered me so that my feet were back on the ground but kept his arms around me. He slumped back against a tree so that we were eye-to-eye, nose-to-nose, and body-to-body, me standing between his legs.

My gaze roamed over his handsome face. His eyes sparkled with the light of a million stars. And that was an honest-to-goodness smile on his face. How could I tell him I was breaking up when he looked so happy?

"Hey, I know you probably have a big Thanksgiving thing planned with your parents, but what if you came to my house for pie? I want my mom and brother to meet you—the right way. And I don't want to wait 'til that next Monday to see you again."

My heart sank to my knees. He wanted to include me in his family's holiday. I'd told him he was my boyfriend, so he assumed I was his girlfriend. Isn't that what couples did? Shared their holidays?

I could picture it. Nick riding up to my house on his bike, parking right there in the driveway, walking to the door, ringing the bell, my dad welcoming him in with a smile and a handshake, my mom hugging him and pulling him inside. Me hugging him, kissing him, sitting him right next to me at our feast-laden table. Us going to his house later for pie and football on TV, and then later slipping off somewhere to make love before he took me home.

It would be wonderful. But that fantasy would never come true. My parents would never welcome him. They would, however, keep their promise to make his life difficult. I didn't want to break up with Nick, but I would to protect him. Even though it would kill me and hurt him.

"What do you say?"

He was waiting for an answer. And I would give him one. After just one more kiss to say goodbye. I leaned in and kissed him on the mouth with all the love I felt for him. My fingers clung to his hair to hold him close to me while his hands cradled my head and back. His leg slid between mine, and I rocked slowly against him in an erotic rhythm we had perfected over the past few months.

"You've lowered your standards since we broke up, Angela."

The hateful, smirking voice a few feet from us pierced my ears like an ice pick, bursting the bubble of pleasure that had surrounded me. I backed out of Nick's embrace. He moved away from the tree and stood like a bodyguard between me and Tyler and his friend Darius.

"When Reed, here, told me he'd seen you swapping spit with this white trash punk, I wanted to beat the shit out of him for lying. But I see he was right." The ugly smirk on his face told me how he felt about it. "But in honor of what we once meant to each other," he continued, "I'll defend what's left of your reputation. I've wanted to kick his motherfucking ass for a long time anyway, ever since he broke my windows and started giving you rides home."

"He's not trash! And he's better than you in every way imaginable," I said, my anger at Tyler's interruption, my anger at having to leave Nick, my anger at my parents for forcing it, my anger at myself for not fighting for Nick sharpened the seething tone of my words.

Tyler's face turned cherry red, except for a spot on each cheek that was white. He had a short fuse, and I recognized the signs that he was almost at the end of it.

"Fuck, Angela, you can't seriously be interested in this asshole."

"Get it through your head, Tyler—you're the asshole I'm not interested in."

His eyes crawled over me, and his lip curled like he was disgusted by what he saw. "I had no idea you were such a low-class cunt. You deserve each other."

Nick rushed forward, grabbed Tyler by the neck, and shoved him hard up against a tree, his face in his. I couldn't hear what Nick was saying, but I saw fear in Tyler's eyes. And I thought I saw a glint of steel.

Darius rushed in, ready to double-team him, but Nick kicked back, striking him in the *cojones*. Darius crumpled to the ground, moaning and clutching himself.

I had to stop this. Nick could get kicked out for fighting, even though it was in my defense. It would set in motion a chain reaction that would be devastating for his future. And as angry as I was with Tyler, I didn't want him to get hurt.

"Nick, stop!" I called out from behind him. "Let him go."

He ignored me. I stepped forward and put my hands on his back. "It's not worth it. Please let him go."

"I won't fucking tell you again." With those final words, ground between gritted teeth, Nick released Tyler and backed away a few steps. Only after Tyler helped his friend to his feet and helped him hobble away did Nick turn to me.

The look on his face shocked me. His usually

warm, soft green eyes flashed like splinters of hardened steel. His tender mouth, always so ready to smile or kiss, was set in a grim line that could cut diamond. I swear I could almost see flames puffing from his flared nostrils. The overall look was hard, brutal, and violent. This was the side of him the report had described.

I could now add one more piece to the puzzle that was Nick Spencer. The rumors that he was a tough guy, a bad boy, were true; it wasn't just an act. He was a raging protector, willing to do whatever was necessary to protect what he considered *his*. And obviously he considered me his.

"I don't suppose you're in the mood to pick up where we left off." His dry humor and half-smile had returned, despite the slight flush still coloring his face.

But I couldn't return his smile. Fear nagged at me like a splinter under the skin.

"What did you say to him?"

"I reminded him that he needs to watch his mouth when he's around you."

"He could make trouble for you, Nick. Big trouble. You don't know…"

The worried look on my face said all I couldn't say. As if to comfort me, Nick smiled and pulled me into his embrace.

"You can't deny it anymore," he said.

"Deny what?"

"You love me."

My heart lurched—from love, yes, but also from regret, pain, and even a little fear at what I'd just witnessed.

"Why would you think that?" I let him hold me, but I didn't reciprocate.

"You stood up for me just now, and in Wilson's office. You kissed me in front of my mom and in front of your house. You called me your boyfriend. You don't say it, but every time we're together, every time you kiss me, and touch me, I can feel it."

I had to tell him before he was hurt any more. "Nick, I have to be honest with you. I asked you to meet me here to...to break up with you." My heart broke in half at the words, but I kept on. "To tell you to forget everything that's happened between us, to forget us." I stumbled over the words and kept my eyes glued to the purple polish on my toenails. I couldn't face him and stab him at the same time.

"But you didn't break up with me. You kissed me. What does that tell you?"

The roughness in his voice killed me. Ignoring his question and the tears burning my eyes, I went into my rehearsed speech.

"This *thing* between us is tearing me apart. All I think about is the next time we can be together. I don't like the person I've become: lying, sneaking around, missing school, all the friction with my parents...just so we can have sex." I was explaining too much, and it would trip me up. "I can't live like this anymore."

"Fine. Let's stop sneaking around. I never wanted that anyway."

"It's not just that."

"Then what?"

"There are too many problems for us to work. It's better for both of us if we just end it. I'm sorry." I started to walk away. He grabbed my hand to stop me, pull me close. And I didn't pull away.

"The only problem in our *relationship* is that you

won't be honest about your feelings," he said, his eyes tight on mine, his voice just tight, like it was hard to find the words.

"I'm trying to be honest with you, but you won't hear it."

He shook his head. "You love me, Angel. You want to be with me. I *know* it with one hundred percent certainty. You won't admit it to me or to yourself, because you know that if you did, you'd have to admit it to your friends and family. And the thought of that scares the shit out of you."

"That's ridiculous." I wasn't afraid of them. I was afraid of what they'd do. To him. To me.

"They've got you wrapped up in a perfect little package, complete with instructions on how to act, what to feel, what to think, what to say, what to wear, and who to love. You're so damn terrified they won't like you if you break out and show them the real you—the real you who loves someone like me."

He was right, and it both thrilled me and scared me that he was. "You want honesty? Here it is: The sex was fun, but you're not what I want." I almost choked on the lie.

"Bullshit." His eyes narrowed at me as his words sliced out. "I'm exactly what and who you want. And if you keep backing away from what you really want because of what others think, you're never going to get what you need to make you happy. And that's not living."

"I have everything that makes life worth living, now and in the future. I'm very happy."

"Liar."

"Okay, right. I *was* happy until you came along and

flipped my world on its side, constantly making me feel like I'm hanging off the edge of a cliff."

"You say it like it's a bad thing. Before you met me, had a single kiss or touch made your heart race a million miles a minute? Had making love ever made you feel like every cell of you was on fire?"

Put your bitch on now before you admit that he's right, about everything, and cave! "Wow! What an ego!" I forced out a rough scoffing laugh.

"With me you're free to be who you really are. The real you comes out every time we're together, every time we kiss, every time we make love. You don't hold back. You do what you need to be happy and satisfied. And that's because of me. Because you're with me. Because I love you. Because *you* love *me*."

God, he knew me so well. It was exhausting trying to be what I wasn't. With him I didn't have to pretend. I could be who I really was, and it was such a gift.

"Don't think that just because we have sex you know me." I had to get away from him before I fell into his arms and admitted that everything he'd said was right and to forget every stupid thing I'd said. "This is pointless," I added, my breath lacy, and started to walk away.

He gripped my arms in his big hands to stop me, his fingers digging into my flesh even through the thick sweater I wore. This time he pulled me in to face him.

"It's not *sex*, Angel. And it's not *fucking*. It's *making love*. And it brings out the best in us. Even though we don't know everything there is to know about each other yet, it's like we've been together forever. We're one person when we're together, whether we're making love, or talking, or hell, even arguing. Apart, we're just two flawed people searching for something we'll never find. Together we're… Together we're fucking perfect." At my silence, he added, "Tell me I'm wrong. Tell me you don't feel the same way about me. Be honest."

Because it would be futile for me to deny it, I didn't. Not completely. "Physical desire isn't enough to base a relationship on. I want it all, Nick—I need it all—a relationship that's going somewhere, full commitment, trust, love, sex, and a secure future. You're only offering me great sex. And it's not enough."

He looked at me, his jaw chewing my words. He was disappointed in me, he was angry with me, he felt betrayed and sad and hurt. I could hear it in his shredded voice, see it in his pain-filled eyes, almost smell it in the drops of perspiration dotting his forehead.

"I am offering you all those things," he said. "But let's be real…that's not the problem. The problem is that they'd be coming from me. And I'm not what mommy and daddy have in mind for their princess. I won't be able to keep you in furs and diamonds or fly you to Paris on a whim. If that's what you really want, then you're right—you're better off with someone else, someone who's okay with buying his woman's love. Me? All I can do is love you, cherish you, please you in and out of bed. And never hurt you."

I couldn't speak from the tears clogging my throat. He was offering me everything I wanted and needed, and all I had to do in return was to admit—to him, to my parents, to my friends, to the world—my true feelings, that I loved him and would fight for him no matter what. I couldn't do it, and I hated myself for it.

At my silence, he released me and turned his back. He ran his hands over his face and stuck them in his hair and growled. When he turned back to me, his arms were at his sides, his eyes calm and sad.

"Have it your way. I'm tired of this shit. Keep to your safe, little bubble. I guess if you don't expect real happiness from life, you won't be disappointed when you don't get it." He spoke the words calmly, as if all of my hurtful words had simply scratched his thick skin and not plunged into his flesh. But I knew the lies had gone deep. Into both of us.

He shook his head. "The Angel I love is kickass bold and fearless. She knows exactly what she wants and isn't afraid to fight the fight to get it. I don't know who you are…Angela. The saddest thing is, you don't know either."

He turned and stormed across the field. Out of my dead, pitiful, sterile, so-called life. It was then that his words hit me fully, "the Angel I love." He loved me. He did. He'd said it several times now. I hadn't said it to him once.

No. He loved Angel, not Angela, the one who had just ripped out both our hearts and trampled them to pieces on the crispy autumn grass. I had a sinking feeling in the pit of my stomach that I had just made the biggest mistake of my life.

Some say that the sweetest sound to a human is his or her own name. He had called me Angela. It was the saddest thing I'd ever heard.

****

The next day, he and I arrived at our lockers at the same time. He glanced up and met my eyes. I held my breath. He immediately looked away and shut his locker. He sailed past me without saying a word, not even a nod hello, not even a look, like I meant nothing to him. My heart dropped into a long nose dive.

I exhaled a breath ragged with tears. I should have been relieved. Now my parents couldn't hurt him. Now I didn't have to fight the hard fight it would take to be with him.

Yeah, I should have been relieved, but I wasn't. I was sick to my soul.

****

The days blurred into one long stretch of out of focus existence, until we were sitting at a week before Christmas break. The pain and longing hadn't lessened in the two weeks since I'd broken Nick's heart and mine, but it hadn't worsened. Until the day I saw him with someone else.

I had a half a credit of PE to satisfy and, since I wasn't on a sports team, that meant some kind of class. Gena and I chose indoor racquetball because it was right before lunch, giving us time to shower after class and not smell like ass for the rest of the day.

"That's a good look for you," Gena said as we left the courts, headed for the showers, a smile on her face as she took in the mess that was my appearance.

I always played full out, so some of my hair had slipped out of the rubber band holding it back, sweat rolled down my body, soaking my clothes. My face was hot and probably void of the carefully applied makeup I had started the day with.

Somewhere just beneath the surface of my pain, I know she was teasing, but me without Nick had been a raging bitch at school and a sobbing freak at home. I started to sling back a snarky comment along the lines of *bite me, bitch*, but out of the corner of my eye I saw Nick leaving the court facility, and my mind went blank of anything but him. Why was he there? Had he been watching me play? If so, what did that mean?

I told Gena to go on without me, and I rushed out the door to see where he was going. Excitement pulsed through me at the thought that he'd been there watching me and that we might talk again. I just needed that hit of dopamine that touching him would give me. Needed something that would regulate my mood faster than the best drug on the market.

He had joined up with a blonde ho in skinny jeans, four-inch-heeled boots, and a low-cut, body-hugging shirt that left nothing to the imagination. The blonde bitch practically curled herself around him and, as one, they headed toward the parking lot.

I should have been in the showers getting cleaned up for my next class, but I couldn't tear myself away. It was like passing a horrible car wreck—you don't want to look, but you do because you can't help it.

He climbed on his bike and put on his helmet. The blonde bitch climbed on behind him, wrapped her bony arms around his waist, and smashed her milk jugs into his back. I heard her witchy cackle from where I stood, until the growl of the bike drowned it out.

A sharp, hot bolt of jealousy seared into me as I stood there in the cold, the wind freezing the sweat on my body. Maybe I couldn't have him, but I was one hundred percent sure I didn't want anyone else to have him.

I went back in and rushed to the showers to cry out the jealousy, anger, sadness, guilt, and longing swirling inside me. As the water pummeled my skin, I kept telling myself I'd done the right thing—for both of us. I just wished I believed it, felt it.

Nick avoided me all during that last week before Christmas break. To make things worse, he was often with that blonde bitch, who I'd come to call BB. Images of him loving her drove me crazy during the day. Dreams of him loving me drove me wild at night.

****

Gena talked me into going to a party that first night of Christmas break. I went because I thought it would help get my mind off Nick. I was talking to the party's host, Matt, who had graduated from our school two years ago. He was telling me about the fraternity he'd joined in college when he stopped mid-sentence, noticed someone in the crowd, and smiled, holding up his hand.

I turned to see who he was staring at, but the room was too packed.

"Nick," Matt yelled to be heard over the music.

Panic stole my breath when I heard the name he was calling. Surely it wasn't my…

"Nick. Over here," he said.

Then I saw him. Nick. My Nick.

My brain screamed, *no, no, no!* My heart cried *yes, yes, yes!* He saw me too, and he paused for an instant. The look on his face said he was as shaken as I was. I wanted to run to him, throw my arms around him, kiss his mouth, taste him, and pull him upstairs to an empty bedroom so he could bring me back to life.

Jealousy stabbed me when I saw the BB at his side, and I felt the blood boil up into my face, turning it hot and, I was sure, red. I wanted to scratch her eyes out and slap him.

Nick and the BB wove their way through the crowd to where Matt and I stood. As they drew closer, Matt grabbed Nick's hand in a warm clasp and did that chest bump/back pat hug guys do.

"Hey, man. Glad you finally made it."

Nick nodded to the BB. "We had to stop at the store for condoms."

Correction. I wanted to kill both of them right fucking now.

"Come here, Honey Lips." Matt grabbed the BB, pulled her into his arms, and planted a sloppy, wet kiss on her. "Let's go try them out."

My jaw dragging the floor, my eyes bugging out, Matt led Honey Lips by the hand up the stairs. She cooed down to Nick, "Thanks for the ride, Nicky."

I watched them ascend, looked at Nick, and then back up at the couple disappearing around the corner, then back at Nick. Surprise stole my voice.

"Chelsea's not my girlfriend," he said.

Relief and joy washed over me, but I kept my tone coldly bland. "Did I ask?"

The corner of his mouth twitched up into a small smile. "You looked like you were worried about it."

"I couldn't care less about who you do, *Nicky*." Damn. That had sounded really jealous.

By the little half grin he gave me, he heard it too. "She's my cousin. I've been playing taxi since she wrecked her car."

"Hmm." I raised an eyebrow in mock indifference and let my gaze travel the room as if I were bored with the conversation. Nick would have laughed at me had he known I hadn't been able to focus on even one person's face out there because *he* was standing right next to me, taking over my senses.

"When we came in, you were looking at us like you wanted to kill us," he said.

I swear he could read my mind. "You always did have an active imagination."

"Some people think she's my girlfriend."

"Well, who wouldn't with her hanging all over you like she does?"

"I thought you hadn't noticed us?"

Ouch, busted! "Well, I only noticed it tonight because you came in wearing her like stink on a skunk."

"C'mon, Angel. Admit it. You've been watching us. Don't deny it because I've caught you watching. You're jealous." He leaned in, close enough for me to smell the cinnamon gum in his mouth. "You miss me."

I shivered at his words, his nearness. I did miss him. So much. "Don't flatter yourself. You could leave town, never come back, and I wouldn't even notice."

I was a flipping idiot! I have no idea why I said that, and I wanted to take it back the second it tumbled from my mouth. The look that washed across his face had me wanting to cut out my tongue and hand it to him as a sacrificial apology. Before I could take that drastic action, Matt came back downstairs and interjected his body between us.

"Chels wants a beer." Then he looked up to a spot above our heads. "Hey, man, Angela's under the mistletoe—go for it! It's the only way you'll get a kiss from someone like her." He laughed and strode off.

Nick and I looked at each other, emotions zinging between us. I didn't know which of us should be insulted more, me for being called snobby, or Nick for being called not good enough to deserve my kiss.

Then Nick looked up. So did I. Sure enough, there was a massive bunch of green plastic mistletoe hanging above my head. Our eyes met and held. I had wanted Nick's kiss so bad for so long I often felt it warming my lips. Now that I was this close to getting it, I felt anything but warm. My fingertips had gone cold and my heart was pounding in my throat. I was afraid and nervous, like a recovering alcoholic suddenly faced with the possibility of having a drink.

I licked my lips. He licked his. He leaned in, touched those wet lips to mine. Joy blossomed in my chest and spread like sunlight through my veins. His mouth opened on mine, just a little, and he teased the tip of his tongue between my lips. My tongue touched his, and my hands rose, cupped his face to pull him in, kiss him deeper. He pulled back.

"Nick…" I caught myself before I clutched at him to keep him from going.

"Bye, Angela. Merry Christmas," he said and left me standing under the mistletoe. The sweet kiss had come so lightly and gone so quickly it almost seemed like I'd dreamt it.

I watched him head into the crowd. A girl who had graduated a couple of years ahead of me grabbed him and wrapped her arms around him, pressed her body against his, and gave him a sloppy kiss. And he didn't stop her. In fact, his arm went around her. The two other girls with her were really happy to see him too, and they each took a turn kissing the guy I was in love with.

I wanted to storm over to them and pull him out of

their arms and drag him outside and make him kiss me like that, make him fuck me like he used to. But I didn't have the right. So instead, I tore away my gaze and went to find Gena. She was having fun and wanted to stay awhile, so after making sure she had a ride, I went home, feeling empty and alone, my heart a frozen mass in my chest.

Nick didn't come back to school in January. I didn't have the courage to ask anyone why. I drove by his house a few dozen times at different times of day. His motorcycle was never there. I saw his brother and his mother, but Nick was never with them. I even called his work; the guy who answered said he didn't work there anymore.

He was gone. Where? Why? Why didn't he tell me goodbye?

What a laugh he'd have, knowing that I *had* noticed he was gone, and that I *did* miss him, and would have given anything to have him back in my life and to be able to tell him the truth: *I love you, Nick Spencer.*

Chapter Nine

The last semester of my senior year in high school should have been one of the most exciting times in my life. Instead it was filled with sadness and regret.

Tyler told everyone about Nick and me and about Nick's past, sprinkling in a few salacious lies to make it juicier, which lost me some friends; not the ones who were genuine, like Gena, but it crippled my once vigorous social life. I didn't date, either, but not for lack of invitations. In fact, the male population at school suddenly had a great interest in me. I turned them all down because I was pretty sure they were only interested in finding out whether I'd do with them what I reportedly had done with Nick. But it was also because I wasn't interested in anyone but Nick.

After graduation I forced myself to take a two-month study abroad class in Ireland, just to get away from everyone and everything. I came home happier than I'd been in a long while and just in time to say goodbye to Gena and get ready to head to college.

I'd been accepted to the prestigious Boston-area university I'd wanted to attend since I was twelve, but when I got back from Ireland, I turned it down, primarily because a large portion of my graduating class was going there.

I instead chose a university where I was sure I'd know no one from home. I wanted to reinvent myself.

Learn to be someone more like the woman Nick had loved. More like the person I knew I was and wanted to be. I couldn't do it in a place where everyone knew my story and would expect me to be that and never change, or constantly compare the old Angela with the new Angie.

Gena got into a prominent West Coast school. She loved the water and couldn't wait to hit the sunny beaches of California. We had been best friends since grade school and had been through almost everything together. And now we were saying goodbye. It was two weeks before school started, and all her essential possessions were carefully stacked in the rented moving van. She and I were in her room, packing the clothes she wanted to take.

"Do me a favor?" she asked as I packed her assortments of scarves.

"Of course," I said.

A sly little grin prefaced her request. "Tell me what was going on between you and Nick."

"Nick Spencer." I said his name softly because it still hurt to say it aloud. I sat still, my head down, my eyes seeing Nick's face in the multicolored pattern in the scarf I clutched in my hand.

"There was a time we told each other everything," she said, hurt in her voice.

I looked her straight in the eyes, my chin lifted. "Nick and I were lovers." I meant to inject pride into my voice, and I was happy at how well I'd succeeded. I sounded strong. I sounded glad to have been his lover.

Gena's eyes grew round with surprise. "Oh. How did it happen?"

"You remember that day I told you Tyler and I

broke up?" At her nod, I continued. "Well after the dance the night before, we were parked at the river. He wanted to have sex but I didn't want to because—"

"Let me guess...he'd been drinking?"

"Exactly. I got out of the car to get away from him and hid in the bushes. He tried to find me but when he couldn't—you remember he had his cast on then—he left me there. I was getting ready to make my way back home when Nick appeared."

"And..."

"And it turned out to be best night of my life."

"So, he's good with his equipment?"

I grinned, dropping my eyes. "Good doesn't even begin to describe his abilities."

Her eyes and mouth rounded into a silent WOW! "I don't understand why you kept your relationship secret."

"He wanted us to be open about it. I'm the one who insisted we keep it secret. I broke it off when my parents found out about us and threatened to make his life miserable. I didn't tell him that. I just let him think it was because I was, like he said, scared by what my friends and family would think of me for being with him. And I guess I was. I mean, I couldn't even tell you, and I could tell you everything. He said I'd never be happy if I didn't start taking chances and be who I really was and not what others wanted me to be. Why are you nodding your head?"

"You've always worried way too much about what other people think."

I nodded. "I've always been comfortable with the rules. I could count on them to give me answers, keep me safe. I wanted Nick, but the rules were very clear about guys like him. He was right when he said I was afraid of what others would think of me, of him, of our relationship. And I was right when I said what would happen if people knew about us. You heard what Tyler said, and you saw how people treated me afterward. Just think what they'd have done to Nick."

"My grandma always said, 'Worry more about what you think of you and less about what others think of you.' So what if people said anything bad about you and Nick being together. If you loved him, you'd have been better off concentrating on what he thought about you and what you thought about him and on building your relationship."

"I was so happy with him. I could be me. I never had to pretend with him. Other than you, he's the only person who got me. And now he's gone."

"Yeah, I noticed he wasn't around after Christmas. Do you know why? Or where he is?

"Not a clue. I wish I did."

"If he were here now, what would you do?"

"I'd ask him to forgive me for being so stupid and to take me back. I'd proudly call him my boyfriend. I'd do everything I could to make it up to him for all the pain I caused him."

She leaned over and hugged me. "I'm really sorry, Angie."

"Me too."

We talked and laughed late into the night. Early the next morning, I said a tearful goodbye to my best friend and started my own packing.

Chapter Ten

I said I wanted anonymity, but after a week of it, trying to meet new people, smiling my face off, telling select parts of my life story over and over again, I swore I'd give up half my future inheritance just to see a familiar face at college.

Fortunately, my roommate had gone there the semester before, and she graciously pulled me along with her and her friends. But I missed Gena. I missed Nick. I even missed Tyler, who already knew me and my story like his own. But I refused to give up trying to build a happy new life that was as far away from Angela as possible. Which is how Angie ended up at the dorms' get-acquainted dance the Saturday before classes began.

The tall blond—Travis—who had attached himself to me from almost the moment I'd arrived, led me off the dance floor, his hand at my back, after we'd danced the last few songs together. He was cute and seemed smart and nice, but his constant talk about that zombie series freaked me out a little. So did the erection he'd sported in his jeans since we'd started dancing. I'm sure it was very nice too, but I wasn't looking for that kind of fun tonight.

I hadn't traded in my number one vice for a new one, I was just taking a break, trying to get myself squared away before allowing someone in again, and I definitely was going to go slow this time. I wouldn't change a thing about my first night with Nick, except maybe to have gone home with him like he'd asked me to, but I didn't want to be the girl whose modus operandi was sleeping with strangers or a series of one-night stands. Not that there was anything wrong with that. It just wasn't who I wanted to be. I wanted something deeper, like what I was on my way to having with Nick before I screwed it up.

"There's punch. Want some?" Travis asked.

"Yeah, that'd be great."

"I'll be right back. Don't go anywhere," he said with a grin.

"Thanks." I smiled but made no promises.

I watched the couples dancing to a slow song the band played. Made me wish I was out there with someone special. Someone like—

As my thoughts showed me Nick's face, I felt a pair of hands settle lightly at my hips.

"I thought the jerkwad would never leave."

The voice that whispered in my ear paralyzed me, locking me in place and stealing my breath, making my heart flip up into my throat.

Oh, God! I knew that voice.

Nick. His name heated my blood, heated my face, my body.

He was here. Behind me. His hands on my hips. His cinnamon breath on my cheek. His body against mine.

Knowing that it was him still didn't prepare me for the soft touch of his green eyes on my face, the sexy grin of his full mouth, the scent of his body when I found the strength to turn around.

Memories rushed through me when our gaze met, memories of how we'd loved each other. He was really here, right here in front of me, and it was all I could do not to fall into him, wrap myself around him, bury my face in his neck, touch his hair, his face, stroke my hands down his chest and feel his heartbeat, take his lips with mine and never, ever let go again.

I'd played out in my head dozens of scenarios of our meeting again, and in none of them had I been too blown away to speak. In none of them had I been shaking and on the verge of collapsing from the joy radiating through my body at seeing him. By the way his gaze held mine, I knew he was there with me in our memories.

"Too shocked to speak, or have you forgotten my name already?" he said.

My lips moved to speak but nothing came out, and I probably looked like a stupid goldfish. Glub, glub. Going on the axiom that actions speak louder than words, I reached out my hand and touched his cheek. A little buzz of energy entered my fingers where the tips met his skin, then zinged up my arm, going straight to my heart. It was great. But it wasn't enough.

"Nick." His name was all I could get out, and that was in a whisper so low that it hardly counted as speaking. But he heard me. I could tell by the way his eyes sparked, by the uneven rise and fall of his chest, by the way he inched a breath closer to me.

I leaned into him and slid my arms around his neck. His arms went around me at the same time and pulled me in tight against his body. We held each other, absorbed each other, and it felt like I was whole again, alive.

How could this be? Was he going to this school? Was it possible that out of all the colleges I could have chosen, I'd chosen the one where he was? A higher power was looking out for me. Or torturing me. I wouldn't know which until this night ended.

When I realized my hand had slid up into his hair and was clinging, realized my other hand had fisted the back of his T-shirt in an iron grip, I slowly stepped out of his arms and looked at him, smiled so I wouldn't cry. I wanted to pinch him just to make sure he was real and this wasn't just some sick joke the universe was playing on me as punishment for hurting him.

Nick grinned at me too, that grin that never failed to ignite the flame inside me, and I knew it was true. He was here. With me. And that feeling raging through me, making every cell in my body dance, was happiness.

I saw Travis coming back toward me, a cup of punch in each hand. Nick saw him too. He took my hand, led me onto the dance floor, and I went with him eagerly. I let him pull me into his arms, happily. My face flushed under his direct stare, and I couldn't stop smiling.

I licked my lips. "I can't believe you're here."

"Yeah, I can imagine that 'an institution of higher learning' was the last place you thought you'd find me."

"I don't recall you mentioning an interest in college."

"I don't recall you asking."

Of course, we were usually too busy doing things other than talking, at least about anything other than the moment, when we were together. He didn't say it, but I could read it in his eyes. His grin told me he could read the same thought in mine as well.

"Well, I'm glad you're here," I said.

"You're glad to see me?"

"I meant I'm glad you're going to college."

"So you're not glad to see me?"

"Yes, I'm…God, you haven't changed," I teased. "You still like to twist everything I say just so you can watch me get flustered. And then laugh at me."

He laughed. "That's what you loved most about me."

I laughed too. "Not even close."

"Are you here visiting someone?" He nodded toward Travis, who was standing at the edge of the dance floor, watching me dance with Nick, glowering. I felt bad for ditching him, but I would have ditched just about anybody for Nick.

"No, I'm going to school here."

"You were headed to Boston. How'd you end up here?" he asked.

He remembered. "Plans changed. How about you?"

"This place offered decent financial aid, and it's a few hours from home, in case my mom and brother need help."

Of course. "Speaking of your family, there's a question I've been dying to ask you."

"Ask."

"It's about that day your mom and brother caught us in bed together."

He smiled, nodded. "I remember that day well. I thought it was going to be my last day on earth."

"What happened when you got home from work?"

"She yelled at me for an hour straight. Cried for ten minutes. Sent me to bed without dinner. Then woke me up, got me dinner, and lectured me while I ate about the stupid choices I was making."

"You mean me?"

"She reminded me how important it was that I focus on school and not let anything—or anyone—distract me. It didn't help my case that the school had sent her my attendance records, highlighting the days I'd ditched class to sleep with my girlfriend...friend... friend with benefits? Whatever it was you were to me."

"Let's go with 'girlfriend.'"

"Hey. I finally have an answer for the question, 'who was your high school girlfriend?' Unless you still want me to keep that a secret." His eyes danced over my face in a heated gaze. The corner of his full lips tipped up in a slight teasing grin that reminded me how much I wanted his mouth on mine. I think I actually blushed at his mention of our agreement. My face heated, and I couldn't stop a grin from taking over my mouth.

"No. I don't do secrets anymore."

One after one, the songs ended, but Nick and I stayed on the dance floor, holding each other, moving slowly in each other's arms no matter the tempo of the music, talking and reminiscing. He smelled so good, felt so familiar, and I never wanted to leave his side.

"Why didn't you come back to school after Christmas break?" I asked.

"You noticed." His eyebrows shot up in surprise.

"Of course I did."

"You told me you wouldn't notice if I left town and never came back."

"I lied. Now tell me why you left."

"I had enough credits to graduate and no reason to

stay, so I kept to my original plan and started college in January."

That part about his not having a reason to stay hit me hard. There it was, as I'd always suspected—he left because of me.

I was about to ask him about his major when the music stopped completely, the lights came up, and the band started thanking everyone for coming out to hear them play. The party planners began picking up used cups, pulling down decorations, packing up supplies.

"That's it?" I asked, still in Nick's arms and unwilling to leave them. "It's barely ten."

"Yeah, these dorm dances are pretty lame, but it's something to do until the parties start." He let me go but took my hands in his, linked our fingers. "What are you doing after this? SAE is usually pretty rocking."

"I thought I'd go home, get my stuff ready for Monday."

He laughed, and it felt like he was laughing at me.

"Why is that funny?" I asked.

"I figured I'd broken you of all your good-girl habits."

"For all you know, Spencer, I could be going back to my room for a *different* kind of party. Something a little more…" I let my eyes dart to Travis, who was still watching us, then let them crawl back to Nick. "…intimate."

He scoffed. "Who with? That asswipe who's been watching you the entire time we've been dancing, holding your little cup of pink punch in his hand like he thinks you're coming back for it, and wishing he had the balls to come out here and take you away from me?"

I said nothing, just let the slow grin taking over my lips say it all.

"Oh, hell no," he said, shaking his head and laughing. "If you're going home, I'm the one who'll be taking you there. What dorm are you in?"

I chuckled at his reaction. Jealousy? Protectiveness? "Redondo."

"Princess Angela's living in the most ghetto dorm on campus? What, did Mommy and Daddy cut you off as punishment for fucking me?"

Truth was, I'd registered so late, it was the only dorm that had any open rooms. But I felt the need to tease him a little too. I let the smile drop from my face and my eyes darted from his. "Well," I started, then just shrugged, tilted my head, suggesting that I was agreeing with him.

My look wiped the grin from his face as easily as marker from a whiteboard. Poor guy looked like he'd been stabbed.

"Angel. I don't know what to say. I'm sorry."

His voice was so soft, his eyes so full of concern, I felt like an ass for deceiving him.

"God, Nick, I'm just kidding. Way to make me feel like a heartless bitch, though."

"Just for that, I'm going to pick you up, throw you over my shoulder, and spank your ass as I carry you out of here."

"You wouldn't."

"I would. And you know it."

Before I could move away, he bent and put his arms around my thighs, lifted me up. My hands reached out and grabbed his shoulders to steady myself. Giggling, I looked down into his face. "Put me down.

I'm probably showing everyone my ass."

"I like you right here," he said.

The way he held me positioned my pussy right at his mouth, and he pressed his nose in, just a bit. The move was so subtle, I doubt anyone saw it but me, but my pussy felt it, and she wanted more. She wanted me to lift my dress higher so his mouth, his tongue, could dive in deep.

The hot way he looked at me made me think he wanted the same thing. He let me slide down his body, slowly, and I felt my dress riding up. He released me when my feet were on the floor, and I settled my dress back into place, hoping I hadn't given the room a look at my cheeky pink lace panties. I glanced around to see whether anyone was watching us and saw Travis toss our cups of punch into the trash and head toward the door, like he knew I was going home with Nick tonight. *Sorry, Travis. Umm...not.*

Nick took my hand. "C'mon, I'll walk you home," he said.

The full moon cast a silvery net of intimacy around us as it we made our way across the dark campus toward my dorm. In high school, Nick and I had kissed, touched, tasted just about every spot on each other's bodies. But we hadn't done a lot of simple hand-holding. His hand, warm and large around mine, felt comforting and exciting. Having him walking beside me, our bodies brushing against each other, felt safe and exciting. Everything I'd felt for him in high school was still alive and well. I still wanted him.

"So, did you run back to Tyler after I left school?"

"No. I told you I was finished with him the night he hit me."

"The night you and I—"

"Yes."

"Did you date anyone else?"

"No."

"So, I ruined you for anyone else?"

I hesitated to give him an answer.

As if he had read between the spaces in my pause, he stopped and turned me to face him. "Tell me."

I took a deep breath, released it. "The short answer is yes."

"What's the long answer?"

"Tyler told everyone about you—your past—and about our relationship, part truth but mostly lies because he didn't have any facts. I felt like the guys who asked me out were only interested in one thing, so I turned them down. Plus, I really had no interest in anyone at that school."

"Shit. I really fucked up your life." There was that concerned look on his face again. It was sickeningly close to pity. "I'm sor—"

"No," I insisted. He did not fuck up my life. I credited him with making it come alive. I placed my hands on his solid chest. "Let's stop saying that to each other. You and I are sorry for any hurtful things we did to each other. I get it. You get it. It's done. We lived through it. Can we agree to no more *sorries*?"

"Agreed."

We kept walking, my hand back in his. We enjoyed a lull in conversation after that, as if we were both lost in those good memories we'd agreed to keep.

"You didn't go to senior prom?"

"No. Did you?" I asked, my voice sharp, bugged that we were still on this track.

"Okay, okay. Don't bite my head off." He said it through a smile, so I know he was only trying to get me flustered...and was happy it had worked.

At my dorm, I thought he'd leave me in the reception area and go on to his party, but to my surprise, he headed to the couches and pulled me along.

"Let's talk awhile," he said and settled in at one corner of a couch.

I sat beside him. The couch was more comfortable than it looked, and the good company made it easier to overlook the strange stains and funky smell.

I worried that sitting had crimped our conversation line, because for the first several seconds, neither of us said a word. Kicking myself for not coming up with something more interesting, I turned toward him, tucking my legs up under me, and tried to get us reconnected using the most common and boring question on campus.

"You didn't say what you're majoring in."

"Mechanical engineering."

"Isn't that like designing engines and machines?"

"Yeah, basically."

"You worked at that motorcycle shop in high school. Is that where you got interested in working with engines?"

His body tensed at my question, taking his posture from comfortable to rigid. His mouth seemed a little tight too, and his eyes moved away from me as if he didn't want me to see what he was feeling or thinking. I'd seen that look before—the time I'd asked about his dad. What would he do this time?

"No," he said. "My dad and I worked on engines together from the time I was little to the time he..."

His sentence trailed off, but I could see in his face that the thought didn't. It was still running around in his mind, poking him.

"It still bothers you to talk about him, doesn't it?"

He turned his eyes back to me. They were shiny, but there wasn't a tear in sight.

"You know, don't you?" he asked.

I nodded. "I'd like to hear your side." His arm lay along the top of the couch, his hand dangling off the edge, close to me. I took it in mine and pulled it into my lap, squeezed it. "If you want to tell me."

He paused so long I thought he wasn't going to tell me. Then he spoke, his voice tired, low, as if telling the story of his ordeal was as exhausting as the odyssey itself had been.

"I haven't told that story for over five years, and even then it was to cops, doctors, shrinks, lawyers, judges, and only because I had to."

"Maybe telling a friend is what you need most."

"You may not be a friend once you hear the whole story."

In high school, that might have been true. After all, part of the reason I had broken up with him was all the stuff in that report my mom had thrust down my throat. But now? I knew I wasn't going anywhere. That period of time I'd been with Nick, and even the time after he left high school, changed me. Love for him slashed my ability to judge him harshly. Still holding his hand, I shifted on the couch so that we sat within the tight bubble of whispering distance.

"You can't get rid of me that easily, Spencer. Spill."

After a moment—of gathering his thoughts, of

searching my face for truths—he began.

"He was my hero. Big, tall, always laughing, talking in this booming voice. We'd build things together. Models when I was little, then later, lawn mower engines, then motorcycle, car, and truck engines. People always said he was real good with his hands. I thought they were talking about his skills as a mechanic. It wasn't until I was older that I recognized the sly looks that accompanied the compliment and realized they meant something else. I'd hear him and mom fighting about his cheating. I was too young to really understand it, but I knew it upset my mom. I'd catch her crying sometimes, at the kitchen sink or at the washing machine. I'd ask her what's wrong. She'd swipe her tears away quickly, insist that she was okay. But she wasn't okay. He cheated on her. With lots of women. And it was killing her. She stayed for us. Simon and me. He told her he'd never let her have us."

He was replaying it all in his mind. I could see it. He hadn't blinked. His pitch hadn't altered. The only movement was his mouth, and his hand which sometimes squeezed mine. Mesmerized, I watched him, listened to him, felt the emotions flowing out on his voice.

"I'd been on a football league team since I was seven. The last season before I started high school, the varsity football coach came out to watch some of my games. He invited me, unofficially, of course, to drop by his practices, toss the ball around. It was the best day of my life, to that point. I convinced my mom to go to the mechanic shop right afterward so I could tell my dad the news. When we got there, I jumped out of the car even before it was in park. The bays were dark, but a light was coming from his office. I ran there, pushed open the door. A naked woman was on top of him, bouncing on him like he was a fucking pogo stick."

"Did he see you?"

"Oh, yeah. He started yelling, 'what the hell are you doing here,' 'get the fuck out.' I ran out of the building. Ran the whole way home. About five miles. Stopped twice to throw up."

I hadn't imagined I'd feel so much pain listening to his story. Tears filled my eyes at the young boy's world shattering around him. I sniffed quietly.

"Are you crying?" he asked in a light, teasing tone. "If you're crying already, I'm going to stop here."

"Me crying? No way. You threw up twice. Cool. And..." I sniffed again and swiped a knuckle across the pooled tears in my lashes before they fell onto my cheek.

He reached out and wiped away the rest of my tears with his thumb. "Sure you want me to go on?"

I nodded.

He kicked back on the couch, laying his head on the end pillow, and held out his arm so I could lie down beside him. Did he need the contact? I know I did. With his arm around me, my head in the crook of his shoulder, my hand on his heart, he continued.

"When I got home, he and my mom were fighting. Yelling, screaming, crying, cussing. He shouted that he was leaving her and Simon and me for that woman he'd been having sex with. Mom threatened to take him to court and get his money and keep Simon and me from him. I got in between them, tried to stop them, but my dad knocked me in the head." He paused. "Made my ears ring for days."

"Had he ever hit you before that?"

"Not like that," he said. "It enraged my mom, and she came out swinging, scratching my dad's face, pounding on him, kicking him. I guess he got tired of deflecting her blows, because he backhanded her in the face and she fell. She hit her head on the table on the way down, opened a bleeding gash on her temple. She was out. I freaked. I tackled my dad like I'd learned in football practice, punched him—I had bruises for days, on my chest and my arms, my hands, even my stomach from how hard I'd hit him. He was giving it to me right back, despite the fact that I was a kid and smaller than him."

He took a deep, shaky breath, released it, as if trying to keep a rein on his emotions so he could finish, as if dumping the toxins building up in his cellular memory from recalling that event.

I wished I hadn't pushed him to talk. Not because I didn't want to hear, but because talking about his past was so painful for him. I slid my arm around him, holding him close. I wanted to shield him with my body. I wanted to heal him with my love and warmth.

"You don't have to continue if you don't want to."

He turned onto his side so that we faced each other, only inches separating our lips. "I want to. This made me who I am today. I want you to know, because I want you to know me."

His arms were around me, holding me close, and his leg was over mine. I felt protected in our embrace, and I think he did too, like nothing past, present, or future could harm us as long as we were together.

"I want that too." It's what I'd always wanted. I put my hand on his face and brushed my lips against his forehead. "Tell me the rest."

He closed his eyes, as if it were critical that he remember the details correctly. Then he opened them. Swallowed.

"I had always been fascinated by the switchblade he carried. It was small and shiny, made of titanium. To me it looked like a little coffin. The blade came out the top of the handle, not the side, and I thought it was the coolest thing ever."

"The knife you showed me the night we met."

He gave me a small nod and a half smile as if it pleased him I'd remembered.

"He promised me it would be mine when I started high school and got on the football team, and he kept it on top of the bookshelf, so I could see it every day and be sure to work for that goal. That night, I stabbed my father with that knife. He had that real shocked look on his face as he used his *talented* hands to try to stop the life flowing out of him. Blood poured over his hands, down his clothes, onto the floor. Then he clutched his chest, and fell. I was sure I'd killed him. Just as I was sure he'd killed my mother. I called 911, but they were already on their way. A neighbor had called them when the shouting had begun."

"Where was your little brother while all that was going on?"

"Simon had pressed himself into a corner, his knees up to his neck, his hands jammed over his ears. It's his eyes I remember most about him that night. They were glazed over and wide, like they were being held open by that piece of equipment eye doctors use. His breathing was choppy, shallow, like he couldn't get enough air to take a breath. When Dad dropped to the floor, the room went silent. It was the weirdest thing. I remember thinking it was like a giant vacuum had sucked out all the sound in the world. I sat beside my brother, holding him, and waited for the police. All I could think about was how was I going to take care of him with both parents dead."

Listening to Nick, I'd forgotten to breathe. I took a deep breath now, released it slowly. We both held still, quiet. I heard the beat of his heart, felt it pounding beneath my hand. I gave him a minute to catch his breath too, then I prompted him to finish. "Your father died."

"That night. After hours in surgery. The police initially thought it was the knife wounds that killed him, but the medical examiner determined it was a heart attack. The trauma of the fight and of being stabbed may have played a part, but they said his damaged heart would have blown in a matter of weeks. In the eyes of the law I was innocent of his murder. But in other people's eyes, it was a different story."

"Anyone who knew the full story would see you weren't at fault."

He shrugged. "I learned right away that people aren't interested in the full story, only the most scandalous parts of it."

People like me. My parents. The Carringtons. Mr. Wilson. Most of the school. How many more people did he have to let judge him? "I know what you mean."

He looked into my eyes. "There's something else about that night. Something no one knows but me. I want you to know it even though it might change how you feel about me."

My heart overflowed with love for Nick at that

moment. He was opening himself up like he'd never done before. I was scared and exhilarated and happy. "I want to hear it."

"My mom told the police I had stabbed my dad to defend us against his attacks. We had the wounds to back it up, so they believed it. But that wasn't entirely true."

He paused and held me just a little tighter, with his arms and his eyes, as if he were worried I'd bolt at his next confession.

"After he'd knocked my mom out, and I tackled him, he got the better of me and shoved me across the room. I fell into the bookshelf, and most of the stuff fell off, including a vase that broke on my head, cutting a gash in my scalp. The switchblade fell off the shelf too, right into my lap. My head was bleeding and I was dizzy from the blow, but my dad didn't come check on me, he just headed toward the door. I told him he couldn't leave, that I wouldn't let him leave, that he had a responsibility to us. He turned around, glared at me— the coldest, hardest look I'd ever seen from him—and told me, 'fuck you, fuck your mom, fuck your brother.' He picked up his suitcase and kept going. That's when I grabbed the knife and jumped up."

He paused again and swallowed. This was it. The big thing he'd held back from me. It was as if he were having to pull it up from a deep, dark place inside him, and it was a battle to get it out into the light. I kept my eyes on his, kept my arms tight around him, showing him I was there for him. That what he had to say wouldn't change how I felt about him.

"At the moment I stabbed him, he wasn't attacking us. He was leaving us. I stabbed him because he was destroying our family. I stabbed him for all the times he'd hurt my mom and made her cry. I stabbed him for throwing us away like we were garbage."

Cold fear—not of him, but for him—raced through me, chilling my blood. I tucked my face into his shirt, trying not to cry.

"Baby, he attacked you and your mom. You were protecting your family. You were just a *child!*" My voice broke and tears blurred my eyes at the last word. "You deserved better than that. And damn him for not giving it to you."

"You aren't afraid of me, hearing the truth…that I'm a murderer?"

"You're *not* a murderer. It was self-defense. End of story. I'm not afraid of you. I've always felt safe with you, even our first night together when the only thing I knew about you was your name."

We hugged for a long minute, our hearts beating in tandem, our breaths rising and falling in sync, our hands roaming over each other's backs.

"Since you haven't run screaming from my arms, I'll tell you the rest of the story."

"More? Oh my God, I really should have brought a box of tissues with me."

"Use my shirt."

"I will not!"

He chuckled. "You won't need the tissues for this part. The day of my dad's funeral, the woman he was running away with drew a gun on my mom, blaming her for my dad's death. I rushed toward her to stop her—I was the protector of the family now—and we struggled, the gun between us. It went off, and she died right next to my dad's coffin, a bullet in her heart. I killed two people in less than a week, and even though both were in self-defense, it kinda fucked up my head. I got into a lot of trouble after that. I got high and drunk almost every day, I fucked every girl who'd let me, and I did everything I could to inflict pain on everyone around me, to make them hurt as much as I was hurting. But then you probably know all that."

The report I'd read was thorough, but I was sure there was more trouble that hadn't been captured. But who could blame Nick for coping with his loss and pain the way he did. He'd come out of it, which is what mattered.

"Your life was never the same after that, was it?"

"Even after I straightened up, stopped abusing, it was still shit rolling downhill. Until I met you." He brushed my hair back from my face with his hand.

"Thank you for telling me."

He looked like he was going to kiss me. But then he didn't. He stood and helped me up.

"I'll walk you to your room before we fall asleep on this nasty couch."

We walked to the elevator, hand-in-hand. As we rode to the fourth floor, I wondered whether he'd come into my room. Whether we'd make love.

"Which room's yours?" he asked when we'd exited the elevator on my floor.

"Four sixty-nine."

He grinned at the number.

"Don't even say a word," I warned.

He shook his head and made the motion of zipping his smiling lips.

"How did I not see what a troublemaker you are?" I said with a laugh.

"You were blinded by my charm, good looks, and love-making skills."

"If that's what you need to tell yourself, babe, it's okay with me."

We were at my room. The narrow hallway allowed us to stand with less than two feet of space between us. The closeness, along with the poor lighting, made for an intimate moment.

"I think I was the one blinded by you." His voice was no more than a whisper I could feel against my lips.

I leaned back against my door. "What about me blinded you?"

His eyes danced over mine as if remembering it all. "Everything." The single whispered word hung in the air, letting me hear it, see it, taste it, feel it.

I wanted to go into his arms, but I didn't want to push him. Our heart-to-heart had changed something between us. I could feel it. Could be he felt too raw to feel anything else tonight. I would let him decide our next move.

"God, Angel. I'm glad you're here. C'mere."

I moved closer, and my arms went around his neck at the same time his arms went around my waist. He eased me even closer into to him. I breathed him in, filling my lungs full for the first time since the last time I'd loved him. I touched the edges of his dark, thick hair, and remembered when I'd had the freedom to grab hold of it during the many orgasmic moments he gave me. It would be so easy to crawl back into our roles as lovers. We were steps from it. I was ready for it. And I think he was too.

Slowly he moved back, dropped his arms to his

sides, pulling himself out of me.

"Wanna come in?" I asked, praying he'd say yes.

"I better not," he whispered.

"Why?"

He took my hand, kissed my palm. "Goodnight, Angel."

He released my hand but I caught his before he stepped away. The words in my mouth tasted needy and I knew they'd sound that way too, but I had to say them. "Don't go. Stay with me."

He searched my eyes, my face, for what felt like an eternity. "I don't have any condoms with me," he said finally. I loved that he knew why I wanted him to stay without my having to say it.

"My roommate has some. She wouldn't mind if we—"

He lunged closer and slid his hands into my hair and held my face as he kissed me. I clutched him to me, wanting to keep him this close to me forever.

"Key," he said.

I gave it to him and continued kissing him as he unlocked the door. As he pulled me into my room. As he shut the door. As he put his arms around me and pulled me in again.

He kissed me deep, sliding his lips over mine, sucking my top lip then bottom into his mouth, his tongue exploring my mouth, teasing my tongue, making up for all the lost time when we didn't have this.

My hands gripped in his hair, pulling his head closer, pressing my mouth closer to his as he pressed his hips hard against me. One hand stayed anchored around me while the other smoothed up my back, found the zipper of my dress and unzipped it, shoving the material from my body. I hadn't worn a bra, so his hand easily found my breast and played while I put my fingers to work undoing his jeans.

I didn't want foreplay. I wanted him inside me, giving me the pleasure I'd done nine long months without. While he shoved off his clothes, shoes, and socks, I pulled off my panties, then rushed to Joni's bedside table, grabbed a handful of condoms from the drawer, and dropped them on the bed. I ripped one open and had it rolled on his cock in seconds. He laid me across the bed, kissed me, touched me, filled me with satisfaction I hadn't experience since the last time I'd been with him.

I spread my legs for him, and he settled between them, positioning his rod against my pussy. I held him at my entrance, and he pushed into me, taking me all at once. Our breathing sped up, our chests falling and rising like we were out of air and grasping for even the tiniest breath. But we didn't shift away from each other, just kissed harder, deeper, devouring each other.

His hips grinding against me, I took him all and urged him to go faster, harder. I was close, and I could tell he was too by his hard, fast, steady, urgent rhythm.

I couldn't believe I was with Nick again, and the pleasure of it, the pleasure of what we were doing, sent me over the edge. I tensed and arched up against him, coming hard, my lips open and on his, my fingers digging into his ass.

A deep guttural noise exploded from his mouth and he jabbed hard up against me, again and again, releasing everything, growling his pleasure.

We collapsed into each other, trembling, our hearts racing, our lungs fighting to catch breaths in the thick, steamy, sex-filled air. I pulled the scent of him into my lungs, into my skin, and I knew: I had been right the first time I'd made love with Nick Spencer—it was happiness. It was why we belonged together.

I lay in his arms, my head on his chest. "Can you believe we haven't been together in nine months?"

"November, last year, right before Thanksgiving," he said, his thumb drawing circles on my shoulder.

The pain of the day I broke up with him was still fresh for me—and maybe for him too—but not as bad as before, especially since I had him in my bed again.

"I have a secret to tell you too," I said, my voice still shaky. "No one knows but me."

"Oh, yeah?"

"You can't laugh, though."

He grinned. "No promises."

"When you didn't come back to school after Christmas, I drove by your house a few times…okay, a few dozen times…just to see whether your bike was there. It wasn't, of course. I wanted to stop and ask your mom where you were, but I didn't think she'd tell me. In case you don't see it, your mom's a little scary."

He laughed. "She can be intense."

"And I called the bike shop. The guy said you didn't work there anymore. He didn't say why and I didn't ask."

He rolled over onto me, held my face in his hands. "You missed me."

"I missed you, and if you say, 'I told you so,' I might have to twist off one of your body parts."

He kissed me. "I missed you too. I was here at college, my dream coming true, and all I could think about was you and how we left things between us. It pissed me off that there was nothing I could do about it."

"I felt the same way. I told Gena I'd had given anything to make things right between us."

"You mean you actually told someone about us?" he said, a look of surprise on his face.

"I did." I smiled proudly.

"What did she say?"

"She said that I worry too much about what other people think, and that I was stupid for keeping you a secret."

"Smart girl, that Gena."

I giggled and accepted his kisses.

In high school, Nick and I had been as physically intimate as two people can be. But this night, I felt closer to him than I ever had. I understood him better. I loved him more than I ever had. My last thought after we made love again and before I fell asleep in his arms was that I wanted to be with him the rest of my life.

****

I woke the next morning alone. Jolting upright, I saw Nick sitting at the end of my bed, fully clothed, even his shoes on. Arms propped on his knees, his head was down, gaze to the floor.

"Good morning," I whispered sleepily.

He slid his gaze my way. "Hey." His voice was flat.

"Why are your clothes on?" I crawled toward him and wrapped my arms around him, kissing his neck. "We have lots more condoms to get through."

He stood. "I have some things to do this morning."

"Okay. Give me an hour to get ready, and we can do them together," I suggested.

"Nah, it's stuff I need to do alone." He walked toward the door as he spoke, like he couldn't wait to get out of there. Was this a brush off?

"Are you okay?" I asked.

His gaze touched me then slid away. "Yeah, I'm fine. Hey, let's have lunch later."

"Sure. What time?"

"Umm, later," he said with a shrug. "I'll call you."

His hand was on the door knob. He really was going to leave. And he didn't have my number. Hadn't asked for it. Hadn't kissed me good morning or goodbye. This was a brush off.

"Nick," I said, and he stopped.

I got out of bed and walked over to him. I knew that look on his face. I'd seen it before. He was pulling away from me. I thought he'd revealed his big secret. Was there another one? I wouldn't push him, but I wasn't going to let him slip away either. I slid my arms around him, hugging him. After a pause, he hugged me back.

"I'm happy we're getting a second chance with each other," I said. "Things will be different this time. Better. So much better. I promise. No stupid conditions. No secrets."

The odd look crawling all over him intensified. I wanted to ask him what it meant, but he didn't look like he was in the sharing mood, and part of me was afraid to hear the answer. Maybe he didn't want to pick up where we left off. Maybe last night had been a one-night stand.

He leaned in and kissed my forehead. My forehead! Shit! I knew what that meant: "I like you, but I don't like you enough."

"See you later," he said, almost as an afterthought as he pulled out of my arms, turned, and walked out.

I stayed at my door, watching him walk down the hall. I watched him push through the door that would take him upstairs to his room. He never looked back. I closed the door to get ready for a lunch that I wasn't convinced would actually happen. This was not how I'd seen our first morning-after playing out.

Chapter Eleven

The best way to describe our lunch that day was to call it the first day of the rest of our *friendship*. We walked to class together, we ate together, we did our laundry together, we studied together, and we partied together. He was careful to keep things easy between us and very platonic. We held hands some—at my initiation—but after a bit, he pulled his hand away. We hugged each other hello and goodbye, but there was no intimate touching, no kissing, and he always came up with some lame excuse for why we couldn't have sex.

I wasn't interested in any other guy but Nick but was annoyed he acted like the big brother, doing everything to keep the guys at bay. We were strengthening our friendship, learning more about each other, but I was frustrated at what was lacking: sex, passion, love.

He'd dragged me to the fraternity parties every weekend since the night we'd made love, and I wasn't happy about it, but my suggestions that we do something different were met with more excuses. But I wanted to be with Nick, so I went.

For the most part, he kept me right at his side, watching out for me. His one-or-two-beer limit at the first party had increased at every party after that. People went to the parties to get shwasted, get fucked, and get unwound. I knew that. But I wasn't much of a drinker, and watching people get stupid and vomit all over the place got old real quick.

Tonight, some of Nick's friends had pulled him into some drinking game, and the group was getting louder, drunker, rowdier, and coarser as time passed. At nearly two in the morning, when he showed no signs of wanting to leave, I said goodbye to my remaining small group of friends and went to check on him and try to get him to come home with me.

I came up behind him and put my arms around his waist. "You guys are having way too much fun over here."

He grinned over his shoulder at me and pulled me around into his arms, kissing my forehead. His eyes were glazed over, and he reeked of beer and pot. "No such thing as too much fun, Angel."

"Or too much pussy," came the cheer from the group followed by laughter at their own brilliance. One of the guys staggered into Nick, making him stagger into me. I caught him before he fell.

"Whoa. I think it's time we called it a night," I said as he righted himself.

The guys booed, and I heard a chorus of retorts from "It's early," to "You're not his mom."

Before Nick could reply, Luke Walker, one of the frat brothers Nick had introduced me to, with a strong warning to watch out for him because he was a dog, was suddenly right beside me, his arm around me. "I'll give you a ride home, Angie."

I wouldn't get into a car with Luke unless I had a weapon, but before I could politely decline his offer, Nick got between us and up in Luke's face, his chest bumping his.

"You're not giving her anything."

"Your *friend* has a mouth," Luke said. "Let her speak for herself." The words themselves were relatively harmless. It was the tone and the smirk that accompanied them that pissed Nick off.

"Back the fuck off, asshole," he growled.

"Is she your girlfriend?" Luke challenged.

Nick said nothing. Nothing. Just as I suspected. We were friends, nothing more.

"Cuz, if she is, I'll back off. But if she's not," Luke said, his tone sharp, "you're the one who needs to back the fuck off."

Nick shoved Luke, hard. Luke stumbled back, the wall catching him before he fell. Nick rushed forward, fists ready, but the other guys grabbed hold of him, trying to calm him down. He flung off his friends, but they blocked him from going after Luke, and I rushed forward, taking his hand.

"Nick, would you take me home?" I asked.

His head whipped around toward me. "I'm not ready to go home."

I'd spent most of high school watching Tyler get drunk and act like an ass. I wasn't going to do it in college, and not with Nick. If this was how he wanted to live, I couldn't be a part of it. I turned away, leaving him, leaving the house.

He caught up with me outside and grabbed my arm. "Where're you going?"

I pulled away and kept walking. "Home."

"It's two in the fucking morning. You can't walk home alone. It's not safe."

I grabbed his hand. "Then walk with me. Come home with me, Nick. Sleep with me tonight."

He pulled his hand away.

I turned again and kept walking toward home.

"Damn it, Angel. Stop!" He was right beside me, and he was pissed.

"Go back to your party," I said. I was pissed too.

"I'm not letting you walk home alone."

"Whatever."

The anger fueling me made my strides fast and furious. He kept up, but a few minutes at that vigorous pace and he staggered behind a tree and vomited.

"Beer doesn't taste as good coming up as it did going down, does it?" I said when he rejoined me, wiping his mouth with the back of his hand.

He glared at me. "Don't fucking lecture me."

I wanted to cry. I wanted to scream. I wanted to demand that he tell me what was going on with him, with us. Instead, I started walking again, him beside me, both of us in complete silence. And I slowed down for his sake. Long minutes passed before I popped the question.

"Why don't you want to be with me?"

He spit into the grass. "We're together all the time." He said it like he was angry about it.

"I mean sex. Why aren't we making love all the time like we did in high school?"

His response balled up somewhere in his throat. Or maybe that was more beer wanting to come up. His pale face reflected the pain rolling in his stomach, in his head. In his heart?

"Just tell me," I said, refusing to let him slide out of answering me. "We've been dancing around it since I got here."

"We can't be lovers again."

The weight of those five words crushed me into the sidewalk. "You don't want me anymore?"

"When you broke up with me last year, you said that a relationship takes commitment from both people to work. At the time, I thought it was a bullshit excuse, but after we had sex here that first night, I realized you were right. I can fuck any other girl and not feel bad about leaving her afterward. I can't do that to you because I care about you too much. But I can't commit to you. So I'm not going to fuck you either."

"Why can't you commit to me?"

"Because you don't have it in you to commit yourself to me, and I don't have the strength to play your games again."

"You're wrong, Nick. I *am* committed to you, have been since we made love after the dance. I told you I was happy we were getting a second chance, and I've tried every way I know to show you I mean it. All my free time goes to you, and we're together, in the open, not hiding our relationship. I'm always trying to hold your hand, hug you, kiss you, make love to you. I call you every night before I go to sleep because I want your voice to be the last one I hear. I stay up with you whenever you're pulling an all-nighter and bring you that spray cheese you love and those energy drinks that taste like glue because I want to be supportive. I include you in every plan I make. Whenever something happens, you're the one I want to tell first. I want a committed relationship with you. I want to be your girlfriend, your lover, your partner, and your friend."

"The only reason you want me is that you're horny and I'm familiar."

"If you think that, you don't know me at all."

"Yeah, baby, I remember this game." He yanked me into his arms, the sour stench of beer and vomit on his breath, and ground his stiff cock between my legs, his hands squeezing my ass to pull me harder into it. "You say I don't know you, then I prove I do by fucking you just the way you need to get off, every time. Isn't that right," he said with a sneer.

I got my hands between us and shoved him away. He teetered backward a few steps.

"I know you too," I cried. "I know that every time I get too close to a truth that you're trying to hide, you push me away. Just be honest with me. Tell me the real reason you're acting like this."

"Just because you don't like what I'm saying doesn't mean I'm not being honest."

I looked at him. He looked at me. There was still so much anger and hurt in him over what I'd done in high school. I could hear it in his voice, see it in his bleary eyes, in his unsteady stance. He still didn't trust me with his heart. And I couldn't blame him. But I couldn't be just his friend.

"So this is it? How it ends for us?" I said, swallowing back tears.

His eyes blinked as if he couldn't believe what I'd said. "We can be friends."

"No, baby, we can't. A friend could watch you fall in love with another girl and be happy for you. A friend could talk to you without wanting to kiss you every other word. A friend could spend time with you without wanting to pull you into bed and make love to you. A friend could be just friends with you without having her heart and soul break to pieces because of it."

This was one of those moments where you know

everything is going to change, and your life will be forever divided into what came before and what came after. The night I first made love with Nick was one of those moments. How could the night I said goodbye to him forever *not* be another? I felt it. Did he? If he did, he wasn't saying. He stood there, mute, nothing to say to my outpouring of emotion.

"You'll regret throwing our love away," I said, quietly but sincerely.

"Like *you* did in high school?" His sharp and low words told me I'd been right, that he hadn't forgiven me.

"Yes." I cupped his face in my hands, brushed his mouth with my thumb. "I threw it away, and I've regretted it every day since."

Thankfully, we weren't too far from our dorm now. Needing to be away from him before I broke down into a blubbering mess, I turned and rushed away. He didn't call out my name, and he didn't follow me.

Before I fell asleep that night, I came to the conclusion that this was karma sinking her teeth into my ass for how I'd treated him in high school. I'd hurt him. And now he'd hurt me.

Payback's a bitch, Angela, crowed the taunting voice in my head.

****

I ordered a latte and sat at one of the tables in the food court to do some reading before my first class. I hadn't read more than one paragraph before I felt strong hands grip my shoulders.

"You look like you could use some company."

I turned my head toward the voice. It was Luke. I didn't want company, especially his. "No, thanks."

He plopped down into the chair next to me.

"Have a seat, Luke." Sarcasm dripped from my words, but he ignored it.

"Don't mind if I do." He brought his foot up to rest on the edge of my chair between my knees and pointed his toe disgustingly close to my crotch.

"This one's taken." I pushed his foot off.

He laughed and moved it to the other chair nearby, giving me a clear view of his crotch, where a tent was rising in his gray sweats. I was not in the least turned on by his display and had no qualms about letting him see me roll my eyes.

"You haven't been with Nick at the parties lately. Trouble in paradise?"

"No trouble, no paradise, no interest in watching people vomit."

"C'mon, you can tell me. Nick's been even more of an asshole lately, and I'm sure it's cuz he doesn't have his sweet guardian Angel there to keep him in line. What's up with you two?"

I lifted one eyebrow and gave him a pointed look that said *mind your own business*.

He laughed. "Oh, so you're *that* kind of girl?"

"What kind?"

He leaned in. "The kind who wants to have her secrets kissed out of her."

He was an attractive guy, but the thought of his kisses made my stomach turn. I rolled my eyes again and scoffed. "Ew. Just...ew."

He laughed. "You don't like me much, do you?"

The lascivious grin he sent me almost had me laughing it was so cheesy. "Whatever would give you that idea?" I said, heavy on the sarcasm so maybe he'd get it this time.

"Angie, your resistance is only making me want to try harder to make you see how much you want me."

Oh, Lord! The man was a dog, but he was a diversion to thinking about how miserable I felt from Nick dumping me.

I happened to look up at one point to see Nick standing several feet behind Luke, glaring at us. His cheeks wore a flush that made his eyes burn. By the rhythmic way his jaw was working, I could tell he was gritting his teeth. His tense body reminded me of a coiled snake ready to strike. And that was definitely jealousy oozing from his body.

He saw me looking at him and must have taken that as a signal to approach because he walked to our table and sat next to me. His face was not the mask of fury he had worn a moment ago. It was calm, not a good calm either, but that eerie kind that settles in right before the storm hits.

"Saint Nick," Luke said, shooting him a sly grin. "Don't tell me you decided to skip physics? That's so unlike you."

"It was cancelled."

"Cool, now I can spend the whole hour with this beautiful babe instead of rushing off to class late." Luke eyed me as he spoke.

"Angela has plans. We're studying for a trig test."

We had no such plans. I hadn't talked to him since we broke up more than a week ago. I started to call him on the lie, but my curiosity had me going along with it.

"I don't think she's that interested in your trig plans. She was about to invite me back to her place to show me her tits...oh, sorry, I meant tatts. Tatts."

Luke's grin, gaze, and tone were highly suggestive, but it was more to goad Nick than to entice me.

"In your dreams," I said, but Nick talked on like he hadn't heard or that what I'd said didn't matter.

"Like I said, she and I have plans."

The two faced each other, eyes locked. Luke's gritted teeth behind his grin showed the mental debate taking place in his head. I saw the instant he backed down. His eyes skittered away from Nick's, and his face flushed. He tried to hide it by grinning, and then standing and putting his attention to grabbing his backpack. He looked at me as he slung it over one brawny shoulder.

"When you get bored and need some fun, you have my number." He tossed a final challenging wolfish grin at Nick. Then with a quick, "Later," he sauntered away from the table, leaving us in electrified silence.

As soon as Luke was out of earshot, Nick leaned in toward me. "What the hell are you doing?" he exploded, his voice low, serious, angry. "I told you how he uses women. Is that what you want? To be next?"

"First of all, we were just talking. Second, I have no intention whatsoever of having sex with him. Third, my sex life is none of your business. And fourth, you've made it perfectly clear how you feel about me, so don't act like you care. It's insulting and infuriating." I grabbed my backpack and tossed my coffee cup into the trash.

"I do care." He must have recognized the look of disbelief on my face, because he amended his statement. "I care what happens to you. I don't want anyone to hurt you."

"You're the only one hurting me."

He clamped his mouth closed tight, saying nothing.

His tight-lipped, refusing-to-talk-truthfully bullshit pissed me off and had me releasing a frustrated sigh.

"I can take care of myself, Nick, so back off."

On the verge of tears, I hurried away before he could stop me. I heard him call my name, but I didn't respond. I had to get away. I didn't want him to see me cry. He caught up with me just outside the door by the fountain and grabbed my arm to stop me.

"Angel, wait."

At his touch, and the sound of my name on his lips, my eyes filled with tears. "Let me go."

He did as I asked. "You're upset. Did he do something to you?"

"No! He didn't do anything. You're the one who has me so brain-scrambled that I'm crying even though what I want to do is punch you." *Or fuck you 'til we're both senseless.* The words choked out through the tears.

"Angel," he murmured and with his thumb brushed away the cluster of tears rolling down my face. "Baby, don't cry."

Why is it whenever people say, "don't cry," it makes you want to cry more? I released another choking sob.

He eased me against him, and I gave in. I buried my head in his chest, gripped the back of his shirt, and just cried. It felt so good to be close to him again, hear his voice whispering sweet sounds against my hair, feel his hands on me, smell his heat energizing me. But he didn't want me. He'd made that clear. Sure, he felt sorry for me because I was crying, but he would comfort any friend, any female friend, if she were in this situation. I wasn't special to him anymore, and seeing him only reminded me of that sad fact. And that's why I was crying.

I moved away from his comforting touch and wiped my eyes with my fingertips.

"Are you okay?" he asked softly, rubbing my arm. "Can I get you anything?"

"I'm fine," I said quickly, annoyance in my tone as I dug for a tissue in my backpack.

"Did you really get a tattoo?"

My head snapped up, and I glared at him through watery eyes, biting the inside of my cheek to keep from screaming as his words stabbed me in the heart. We'd shared our feelings on tattoos the first night we met. I thought he knew me better than to ask that question. More evidence that I wasn't special to him. I bit my lip and walked away.

"If you had found something that held that much meaning to you, you'd have told me," he called out, stopping me in my tracks.

He remembered! I wanted to rush back into his arms, kiss him until he admitted he'd been wrong. Admitted he loved me and wanted me back. Knowing he wouldn't, I wiped my teary eyes and my runny nose and rushed on to class.

I had found something that held that much meaning to me. Him. And I had told him. I didn't ink it on my body because it was already inked on my heart. And he was too scared to take the chance to see it.

****

For the next few weeks, I stayed far away from Nick—and Luke. I spent more time with friends, worked out harder to ease my sexual tension, replaced the batteries in my vibrator twice, went to parties that

Nick wasn't going to be at, and focused on my school work. Unfortunately, nothing filled the hole that Nick's absence left.

I missed him so much some days that I couldn't think straight. I missed his smile, his voice, the way he smelled. I missed his presence beside me as we walked together, or sat together studying, eating, talking, laughing. I missed our spirited discussions. I had often thought of the many joyous hours we'd spent making love. Now, I seemed to live there in that memory.

Would I ever learn to live without him? I now understood why he left high school when he did. It was too hard to be around the one you love and not be with them. Maybe I should think about transferring to another school.

****

Joni was out with her boyfriend all weekend, and I was in my room alone, doing homework on a Friday night, wearing nothing but a cami and panties, my hair up in a messy knot, no makeup.

I ignored the knock on my door because, well basically, I looked like shit and I had to finish an online quiz that was due at midnight and I was in the middle of it, with twenty-five minutes to spare. But when the knocks turned to pounding, I jumped out of bed and went to the door.

"What?" I growled as I flung it open.

Nick stood there. My lungs stopped, my heart stopped, and my nipples rose hard against my cami. His eyes crawled over my half-naked body.

"Nick, I'm in the middle of something, so this isn't the best time."

His eyes went hard. "Do you have a guy in there?"

I thought about lying to him, making him jealous, but I didn't want deceit between us. I was tired of secrets and lies.

"I'm taking a quiz."

"We need to talk."

"About?"

"Us."

"There *is* no us," I said with a sigh. "You made that very clear. No need to tell me again."

I started to close the door, and he put his hand on it to stop it. He came in and closed the door behind him. The room immediately got hotter and smaller.

"I told you I'm busy."

"I was wrong," he said. "Wrong and stupid." He took my hand, eased me closer, into his arms. "I love you. I want us to be together, and I'm willing to do whatever it takes to make it happen."

Happiness flooded my body the instant his mouth took mine. He was back where he belonged…in my arms, in my life and, soon, in my bed.

We fell across my bed, kissing, our clothes disappearing off our bodies. His hand moved to my breast and palmed it, tweaking the hard nipple between his fingers. Then it slid down my stomach, dipping ever lower, until it was at my mound, cupping me. His fingers slid between my lips and pressed against my pussy, making me gasp. It had been so long since he'd touched me like this, and I moaned with the exquisite torture of it.

"Open your legs for me, Angel. I want my tongue in you."

I shifted my legs apart and raised my arms over my head, my eyes never leaving his, telling him he could do what he wanted to my body.

He inserted one long finger into my slick, wet pussy and used his thumb to swirl over my clit. My eyes fluttered closed and my mouth parted, releasing the first of many moans of appreciation to come.

Bubbles of pleasure built up and burst inside me as he fingered me in a steady plunging motion. All my focus centered on the dizzying pleasure swirling between my legs. I could see it, smell it, feel it—I was nearly there, to the top.

His mouth moved to nibble my jawline, my neck, my shoulders, my breasts, and little shivers danced in his wake. With his wet tongue he flicked over my needy nipples, faster and faster, until my breasts were so sensitive I thought they would scream. He mouthed the whole nipple and as much of my breast as he could take into his mouth, then sucked. Hard, then gentle. He repeated the action with my other breast before nibbling down my stomach.

The scrape of his lips and teeth and tongue and scruff against my lower stomach made me spread my legs wide for what I knew was coming. He nibbled straight down the center of my pussy, massaging the mound with his mouth, squeezing the outer lips between his lips, sliding his tongue up and down the entire slit, taking his time when I'd rather he take me all.

Digging deeper each pass, he finally plunged between the slick folds to tongue the erect bud, round and round, then the other way, then flicking it back and forth until my head thrashed on the pillow in pleasure. Gently he pressed his tongue inside my pussy and explored and massaged it, feeling up, down, sideways, varying the depth, speed, and pressure, sometimes using just the tip, sometimes going deeper. When his tongue fucked me deep, his top lip teased my clit, and I cried out again, arching against his mouth.

I heard a far-away voice, that sounded like mine, begging him to fuck me. But he wouldn't. He just kept his mouth on me, toying with me, driving me out of my mind with the need to come.

My world became that area where we were connected, that frenzied area of building pleasure, and I felt nothing but that. The tension ratcheted up, tighter and higher. Oh, God! I needed him! Needed his cock inside me. Why wouldn't he give it to me?

I forced my eyes open and looked at him, snatched at his head with my hands to get him to come over me. "Nick. Please. Fuck me."

His mouth stopped, and I wanted to cry at the frantic buzzing need between my legs. He looked up at me, his eyes drunk with pleasure from eating me, my juice covering his face. His lips parted.

"Angel," he whispered.

I groaned, thrusting my hips up and my pussy back to his mouth, trying to make him continue what he'd started. I was breathing hard, about to come apart. I put my hand to my clit to finish the job myself, but he caught it and moved it away. He was torturing me!

"Finish me," I cried out. He just smiled and again said my name, still a whisper but louder this time.

"Nick!"

"Angie," he said. "Get your lazy ass out of that bed."

Suddenly, he was no longer between my legs but was standing over me, grabbing my shoulders and shaking me. All his clothes were on, and he was wearing his motorcycle helmet and black shades.

"Get up," he said. "You need to get ready."

"What?" Anger and confusion and red-hot need shot me upright.

My body jerked, and my eyes popped open to see the grinning face of my roommate standing over me.

"Damn, girl," she said. "That must have been one hell of a wet dream."

I sat up, looked around the room. Nick wasn't there. Just Joni. And me and my throbbing pussy. If she weren't there, my hand would be diving into my panties to finish the dream Nick had started. It had felt so real.

"Shit!" I plopped back down on the bed. "Yeah. It was. And you woke me up. Bitch."

She laughed. "You need to get ready."

"For?" I said, my brain still not functioning.

"The Back to the 80s Prom," she said.

Joni had broken up with her boyfriend and was suddenly eager to go to all the parties and events and drag me with her. I went because it was better than staying home and crying over Nick—and having wet dreams about him, which came more often than I cared to admit.

Nick had asked me to go to the dance with him. Said it would be the prom neither one of us had. I had been looking forward to it. But that was before we'd had our falling out. Now, I had no interest in going. I didn't want to dance with anyone but him, and I knew that wouldn't happen. And I absolutely knew I couldn't stand watching him dance with other girls.

"I've changed my mind," I said. "I'm not going."

"You were looking forward to it before. What

changed your mind?"

I got off the bed and grabbed a bottle of water from the fridge, saying nothing.

"What did he do now?" Joni asked.

"Who?" I guzzled the cold water, and some dribbled down my chin and chest. It felt good on my fevered body, and I was tempted to dump the whole thing down my panties.

"Duh. The only guy who has the ability to send you on a freak-out this ugly."

"He didn't *do* anything. That's the problem." I had told her what had happened between us the last few weeks.

"I told you—he's interested; just scared. You know how into school he is."

"I don't have a problem with that, but it's all he seems to cares about. That and drinking himself numb so he doesn't have to face the truth."

"Here's what I think. He doesn't want to get involved because he's afraid he can't give you the attention you want and deserve, so he instead plays it safe and keeps things friendly. That way, he keeps you near, and he doesn't get hurt again. And, because his stupid plan isn't working too well, he drinks to keep from thinking about how much he wants you."

"If I didn't hate the taste of liquor, I'd take up drinking to forget him and get on with my life. I want him so much it hurts."

"Yeah, I could tell by the way you were moaning and humping in your dream." With a wicked grin, she rubbed her hands over her breasts, thrusting and rotating her hips, and whimpered, "Oh, Nick. Finish me," imitating me.

"Shut up!" I laughed, embarrassed from being busted having a wet dream. "That's the most action I've had in a month. Don't make fun."

She laughed too. "That settles it. We're getting you laid tonight. For reals."

"We are?"

"Yes, so you know what that means."

"Uh…wear nice panties?"

"Nice panties? Aww. Bless your sweet little heart," she said in a sugary, sarcastic drawl. "No, darlin'. Tonight, you're going commando."

"I am not going commando. Especially in that purple skin-tight stud magnet you chose for me."

"Nick's a stud. It'll get his attention."

"No, you forget—I know him. I know how he thinks. He'd see it as proof that I was lying about wanting only him."

"Then wear the pink one. Nothing says *sweet and innocent* and *come eat me* like layers of pink fluff."

"It looks like a pink nightmare, and—"

"Pink or purple—those are your choices. But I swear if you try to put panties on tonight, I'll rip them off you myself. You'll thank me later when he pulls you into a dark corner and hikes up your dress to slip you the big one."

"You're assuming I can even get him into that dark corner."

She grabbed my arms, made me look at her. "All you need to do to get Nick into that corner tonight is to march over to him at the dance and whisper one little sentence in his ear."

Chapter Twelve

The prom was in full swing when Joni and I arrived. Thousands of tiny colorful lights lit up the room like a rainbow and sent a magical sparkling net out over everyone on the dance floor. Women in dresses every color of the flower garden looked like blooms ready to be plucked. Sharp men in black suits, looking manly and handsome and eager to pluck. Odd that I'd seen some of the same guys just last weekend at another party, stripped down to their boxers, doing shots out of the belly buttons of some of the girls. Ah, what a little spit and polish could do.

I danced with several guys while keeping an eye out for Nick. When I saw him standing across the room, watching me, it was all I could do to not race to him and tackle him to the floor and whisper in his ear that sentence Joni had insisted would make him unable to resist me. Instead I accepted Ben's offer to dance. I'm sure I was all over his feet because I couldn't get the picture of Nick out of my head long enough to pay attention to what I was doing.

Nick looked so good. His suit made his shoulders look even broader, his legs even longer and stronger. He was clean shaven, and I wanted to run my mouth over his smooth jaw, chin, cheeks, feel it nuzzling the softest skin on my body. His hair was a little damp, which meant he was fresh from the shower. I bet he smelled really good too. And tasted good. God. That's the guy I wanted.

Before the song was half over, Ben suddenly stopped, looked behind him. Nick was there, tapping him on the shoulder. Ben turned back to me, then let me go as if he could see in my face the desire to be with the intruder.

Nick took my hand, put his arm around my waist, and eased me against his chest. I thought we would dance, but we just stood there, looking at each other, our pounding hearts doing all the talking.

When another song began, Ben was back, tapping Nick on the shoulder, wanting to finish out his dance. I held tight to Nick, wanting to make him stay, but he stepped out of our embrace, releasing my hand. Ben put his arms around me and danced me away from Nick.

Seconds later, Ben stopped again and spun around. "Dude, what's your problem?"

Nick stood behind him. "She's my girlfriend." He said it to Ben, but he looked at me.

"Whatever." Ben let me go. I know he walked away, but I didn't see it. My eyes were filled with Nick.

He took my hand, but instead of taking me in his arms and dancing with me, he led me off the dance floor, out of the building, and down the street to his motorcycle. He took off his suit jacket and put it on me. It was October and chilly, but I didn't feel it with him next to me. He got on his bike, started it. I gathered up my skirts as best I could and climbed on behind him, holding on to his body for dear life. He kicked it into gear, and we sped away from the party.

We said nothing during the ride. He concentrated on the traffic while I concentrated on the feel of my arms holding onto him, of my front cradled into his back. I didn't know where he was going. Or why. I didn't care. I was with him, his heat meshing with mine, and that's all that mattered.

Hugging closer to the familiar body in front of me, I smiled remembering that he'd called me his girlfriend. I buried my grin and my nose into the soft material of his shirt and breathed deeply of his distinctive scent, something I've never been able to describe without sounding like a commercial touting the benefits of a fresh-from-the-shower clean feeling.

He pulled into the parking lot of a park, stopped the bike, and killed the engine. He rocked it up on its stand, and just sat there, gripping the handlebars, silent and still. I rubbed my hands up and down his chest lightly and whispered his name.

He turned his head slightly toward me, but didn't look at me. Enough moonlight shone for me to see the tight set of his mouth. He dismounted and walked a few feet away, sat on one of the benches. I got off the bike and joined him. He'd called me his girlfriend. I'd thought we'd be making out by now. Instead, the tension between us hung heavy and thick as a steel curtain.

"You're so quiet." I put my hand on his knee and stroked up his thigh. "Say something."

"What do you want me to say?" he said.

"You can start with why you brought me here."

"Would you rather have stayed at the dance with those guys all over you?"

Hearing anger in his voice pissed me off. I left the bench and faced him, the frustration of all these weeks without him surging through me. "Don't you dare act

201

like I cheated on you just because I chose to have fun at the dance instead of sitting at home crying over you. I wanted to be there with *you*, but you dumped me."

"You dumped me," he said.

"Are you talking about high school again? God, just get over it."

"No, I'm talking about *here*, weeks ago. When I told you we weren't going to have sex, you stopped hanging out with me. Wouldn't have anything to do with me."

"I told you I can't just be your friend. I want more. And if I can't have it, then…"

"Then what?" he said, his eyes boring into me, his pain showing.

"Then it's best we don't see each other at all. It hurts too much."

"I thought you'd changed since high school, but you haven't," he accused. "It's still all about you. Everything has to be your way or no way."

Anger was front and center in his voice, his mannerisms. Maybe we'd finally get somewhere tonight with this, settle it once and for all.

"Did you bring me out here to lecture me? Tear my heart open again by pretending to care about me when we both know you don't? If that's what this little abduction is about—"

"I do care about you!" He shot to his feet.

"As what…a fellow human being? A friend?"

"Yes."

I scoffed. "That's not enough."

"What the fuck do you want from me, Angel?" he growled. "You want me on my fucking knees, telling you how much I love you? How miserable I am without

202

you? How wrong I was for giving you up?"

"You don't have to be on your knees, but yes. That's what I want. I want you to admit that you love me. I want you to make love to me. I want you to—"

He yanked me up against him, his arms around my back, and crushed his lips against mine, rough with anger, hunger, frustration. Our bodies locked in a steel-tight grip that was more battle than embrace. Mouths punished, teeth bit, tongues stabbed each other.

I wanted him. And by God I was going to have him. My mouth was too busy to say "the sentence," so I went with plan B.

My hands jammed between us and undid his pants, and he didn't stop me. His cock jabbed against his underwear, hard and ready for me. I shoved his pants and underwear down, and he didn't stop me. I grabbed his cock, stroked him, and smeared his pre-cum across his cockhead. And he didn't stop me.

Feeling my own need pooling between my legs, my hungry pussy almost screaming for his cock, I forced him backward until his knees hit the bench and he sat. I lifted my dress the best I could and climbed on him, straddling him, kissing him, all the while trying to pull up the layers of pink still tucked between us. He yanked up material too, until his hand could dive between my legs to shove aside my panties. When he found none, a light flared in his eyes, as if it turned him on that I wasn't wearing any. He centered his rod over my ready cunt and thrust home as I slid down onto him.

"Ah, fuck!" we both said in a long, drawn out moan at the moment he was all in.

When I could see and move again, I gripped the back of the bench and used it to help me ride him, hard, fast, fully. He felt so good, filled me so deep, made me whole, like nothing else could. His hands gripping my bare ass, he bucked into me, matching my sharp stabbing movements.

This was raw, rough fucking, with a single mission—for both of us to come together, as one. I felt the tightness in my stomach gripping and felt my pussy opening up, ready to release. He pounded harder, faster, and suddenly we were both there, growling like a couple of mating animals, my pussy gripping his cock, locking him inside me, his hot cum shooting inside me, branding me as his.

Afterward, I collapsed against him, trembling in his lap, feeling his shaft twitch inside me. Before I could catch my breath, his mouth was back on mine, this kiss passionate, deep, erotic, his hand on the back of my neck holding me closer. Our tense grip had relaxed, but we were still wrapped around each other, so close I wasn't sure we would be able to separate. This was no wet dream. This was real and right.

"Does that tell you how I feel about you?" His whispered voice was ragged. His lips gently stroked over my kiss-plumped lips.

I swallowed the lump of bliss so I could speak. "It tells me a lot, but not enough. Tell me more. Start with why you brought me here."

He kissed me softly on my lips, then helped me climb off of him. It was then that I felt our mingled cum running down my legs and realized we hadn't used a condom. I had started taking birth control pills the day after our first dance, hoping to eventually dispense with the condoms. I hoped he was still clean.

We had nothing to wipe up with, so I sat beside

him and lived with my first wet spot while he fastened his pants.

He leaned over, elbows on his knees, hands together in a teepee, fingers digging into his forehead. Whatever it was he was struggling with, it was chasing him hard.

"I had to get us out of there before I hurt one of those guys for touching you."

"Not one of those guys meant anything to me. You're the only one I wanted to be with tonight. You're the only one I've wanted to be with since I met you."

"I know," he said finally. "It's what I wanted too."

"Then why did you push me away when we were getting our second chance?"

He was quiet for a moment. "You know how I felt about you in high school."

"You said you loved me and wanted a relationship with me."

He nodded. "Before I met you, all I wanted was to get out of that school. I didn't fit in, and I know that most people thought I was nothing more than a loser with no future. What they didn't know was that I had been taking summer classes and testing out of other classes from the time I got kicked out of my second school. There was nothing I wanted more than to graduate early, get on to college, finish, and get a good job with good pay so my family would never go without again."

He sat upright then, turned his head toward me, the anger gone from his eyes, his mouth.

"That all changed the night you and I made love. It's like you owned me that night. I couldn't get you out of my mind. I couldn't get the taste of you out of my mouth. I couldn't get the scent of you off my body. The feel of you off my skin. That last semester was the best and worst time of my life. Being with you was like…it was a great high when we were together, and a hard crash when we weren't. You burned out all thoughts of anything else. All I could think about was being with you again. I almost failed English because of all the days we ditched. The only reason I passed was because of the teacher's kindness and the extra work I put into it after you broke up with me. If I had failed, I could have lost my scholarship to this college."

"Surely one bad grade wouldn't have kept you out?"

"I'm on an academic scholarship, and it was offered based on a good final high school GPA. A failing grade would have lowered my GPA, which might have stripped me of the award, which would have ended my shot."

"You could have made up the class that next semester. They would have done a grade replacement for you."

"I wouldn't have stayed around to make it up. I couldn't stand being so close to you but not being able to talk to you or kiss you or touch you or make love to you. I couldn't stand the thought of seeing you with another guy. I had to get away."

"You did go away, and you never looked back. Never said goodbye."

"Actually, I did say goodbye…at that Christmas party. When you said you wouldn't notice if I left and never came back."

I wanted to dip my head in shame, but I kept my eyes on his. "I didn't mean it. It really hurt when you left. I didn't know where you'd gone, or why. I thought you had just…" I shrugged, not wanting to say aloud what it was I had thought.

"Dropped out? Got kicked out?"

"I just knew that you were gone, and I was sad and angry that I never got the chance to tell you how important you were to me. Why didn't you ever tell me about your college plans?"

"I don't know. Guess I thought you'd laugh at me. Or that I'd jinx it."

The bridge of my nose tickled with tears that he thought I'd laugh at him, at his ambitions. I grabbed his hand. "Baby, I never would have laughed at you. I would have been so proud."

He leaned in and dropped a soft kiss on my mouth. "When I saw you here, at that dance…" He shook his head, grinned. "…God, I was so happy. When you acted like you were glad to see me, I thought that maybe we could pick up where we left off, that maybe being away from your friends and family you wouldn't have the same hang-ups about being seen with me. Then we made love again, with that same intensity between us as before. I was afraid it would overtake me here like it did in high school and derail me. I've got my whole future wrapped up in college. If I mess up, I might not get a second chance."

"So you chose college over us."

He faced me, brought my hand to his mouth, and kissed it. "Yeah. But it was harder than I thought it would be. I drank more and more at the parties, trying to stay high to help me forget how much I wanted you, but it didn't help. Every time I saw some guy talking to you—hell, just looking at you in that way—I went crazy. Seeing you with other guys was more distracting than being with you. Seeing you dancing with those guys tonight made me realize that if I didn't do something soon, if I didn't step up, I'd lose you. I can't let some other guy have you."

"Why?"

"Why? I thought you smart, rich girls had all the answers."

"We do. I just want to hear you say it."

He pulled me into his lap again, wrapped his arms around me, and drew me against him. "In high school, I told you that you needed to take risks to get what you needed to make you happy. Now I'm taking my own advice. I love you, Angel. I want us to be together, and I'm willing to do whatever it takes to make it happen."

"Nick, you are *not* going to fail—not at school, our relationship, or at anything else you want. Maybe I didn't have a lot of faith in us when we were in high school, but I do now. I'm committed to you, to making us work. I want to be there to help you succeed. I want you there for me. Together we'll have everything we want."

"What I wouldn't have given to hear you say that in high school."

"I should have," I said, and reached out to caress his face, trying to rub away the hurt I read in his eyes. "But I'm saying it now. There's something else I should have said out loud a long time ago." I cupped his face in my palms. "I love you, Nick Spencer." I kissed his right eye. "I love you." I kissed his left eye. "I love you." I kissed his mouth.

"Angel," he murmured through our kisses. "I love you too."

"Good," I said. "Now that that's settled, can we go home? I want you in my bed."

"Before we go, there's something I have to ask you."

"What?"

"May I have this dance?"

"You want to dance with me?"

"This is our prom, after all."

I grinned. "We were at our prom. Why didn't you dance with me there?"

"You were so beautiful and perfect in my arms I wanted to stay still, freeze the moment, so I'd never have to let you go again."

His romantic words and gesture touched me in a way nothing ever had before, and my heart swelled with love, so full I could barely speak.

"Yes, you can have this dance and all the others." *For the rest of my life,* I added silently as I went into his arms and danced with my boyfriend, my lover, my best friend.

****

Later, as we rode the elevator to Nick's room, I was thrilled to learn that his roommate was out of town for the entire weekend.

"I plan to keep you naked and in bed the whole time," he said, standing behind me, his arms loose around my waist, his mouth nibbling my neck.

"I'll need to get up and brush my teeth now and then, but other than that, you won't get any arguments from me."

"Fine, but you'll have to use my toothbrush. I'm not letting you out of my room."

"You're lucky I love you so much. Normally,

having to share a toothbrush would be a deal breaker."

He laughed. "And before you ask...Yes, I have condoms. I bought the biggest box I could find, hoping you'd end up with me here eventually."

We stepped off the elevator and walked down the hall to his room.

"Speaking of condoms," I said, "you know we didn't use one tonight."

"Ah, shit, you're right. Do we have anything to worry about?"

"I'm clean and I'm on the pill. What about you? Did you go horn-dog crazy on all the college hos before I got here?"

He didn't answer, giving me my answer. I stopped, faced him. "So, is that a yes on the hos, or a no on the being clean?"

He cupped my face, looked me in the eyes. "I always used a condom. I haven't been with anyone but you since you got here. I'm clean."

My stomach clenched at his admission, and my eyes left his to stare at the gray stain on the wall that looked like a screaming face. It wasn't what I'd hoped to hear, that he'd been with a lot of girls after me, but I couldn't fault him. As far as we both knew, we were done. It was ridiculous and unfair to think that either one of us would remain celibate for very long after we broke up, to think that we wouldn't move on. I'd been with a guy since, so I had no room to judge. What hurt, though, is that he had moved on so quickly.

"Is that another deal breaker?" he asked, his quiet voice shaking me out of my pity party.

I met his eyes. "No. I guess I'm just disappointed you weren't as miserable as I was," I said with a little grin.

"I had sex with them *because* I was miserable without you."

"You're such a guy," I teased and grinned up at him, kissed his mouth.

"And you like me that way." He kissed me back.

"I do."

"You didn't sleep with anyone after me?" he asked with just a little too much pride in his voice.

"There was one guy."

He stopped me. "Who?" Did that tight voice mean this revelation could be a deal breaker for him?

"I went to Ireland for two months over the summer as part of a study-abroad program. Riley was the TA in one of the classes I took. He was clean, and we always used a condom."

"Oh."

"When I lost you, I felt dead inside. For five long months I moped around, not caring about anything. I woke up one day and was just tired of it. I accepted the fact that I'd never get you back. Going to Ireland was my first step toward moving on. Riley was part of that."

"When did you get on the pill?" he asked.

"The Monday after the first time we made love here."

"Really?" he said, smiling.

"Yeah, I skipped my first class and went to student medical for a prescription. I stayed on it even after you cut me off, hoping you'd come to your senses."

"And if I hadn't?"

"You did. That's all that matters."

We were at his door, and he turned to unlock it. "So, you're good with not using condoms?"

I slid my arms around his waist, let one hand lower to his crotch, and cupped him. He was hard again already, and I stroked him. He was taking his damn sweet time with the lock and key, and eagerness flared across my body. "Yes, unless you enjoy having a barrier between us."

"I don't want anything between us," he said.

"Good. Now hurry up and open this fucking door before I break it down."

He laughed and did as I asked.

"Does that pink puff have a zipper?" he asked once we got inside and shut the door.

"Yes." I slipped out of his jacket and slid it around the back of a chair. "But I want you to cut it off me with your switchblade."

His eyes closed halfway, and he grinned. He pulled the knife from his pocket, pointed it in my direction. The blade slid out of the top, the point stopping right at my bust line. The cold sight and sound of it made me shiver. With anticipation.

Chapter Thirteen

"Just don't cut off anything important," I said as Nick's blade slid out.

Grinning, he lowered the tip of the weapon to rest at my waist where the bodice started. He slid the knife up the front of the first gauzy layer, slicing it open easily. The second layer, a lacy material, sliced open as easy as the first.

Going a little deeper for the third and last satin layer, he dug the point in at my waist and flicked upward. A little hole appeared there. I held my breath as he slid the knife into that hole and, slowly and carefully with constant pressure, drew it up, up from my waist, up my stomach, between my breasts, stopping at the very edge of the low sweetheart neckline.

The soft zipping sound of the soft material submitting to the hard blade reverberated over my nipples, my clit. My breasts poked through the gash, the mounded flesh pressing for release.

He retracted the blade and put the knife back in his pocket. His hands grabbed the sides of the cut material and pulled, and the last bit holding together at the neckline gave way. He ripped the skirt material down below the bodice then, right down the middle, and kept ripping until the dress was almost completely split in two and hung on my body by the slim gauzy straps at my shoulders. He eased it from my body and it whispered to the floor in a rustle of fabric.

I stood naked in front of him, the desire and admiration in his thorough gaze tightening and tingling the skin all over my body. I wanted his touch. I wanted to touch him.

I put my hands to the buttons of his shirt. My dress was a cheap, thrift-store find; this shirt cost him good money. Even though I wanted to rip it open like he'd ripped my dress, I undid the buttons one by one. I slid my hands into the part in the shirt and smoothed it over his bare chest, his shoulders, and pushed the shirt down his arms. It joined my dress on the floor. My hands went to his pants.

"Why weren't you wearing panties tonight?" he asked.

I looked up to see him looking at me, a grin on his face. I grinned back and put my hands to work on unbuttoning and unzipping his fly. "My roommate told me that all I needed to do to get you to fuck me again was to march over to you at the dance and whisper one little sentence in your ear."

Unbuttoned and unzipped, his pants slid to the floor with a little shove from me. He kicked out of them and his shoes.

"What sentence was that?" he asked, reaching down to pull off his socks.

My hand went to the hard-and-ready bulge in his boxer briefs, stroked him through the fabric, cupped his balls. In my sexiest voice, I leaned in, my mouth at his ear, and whispered the answer to his question. "I'm not wearing panties."

His cock jumped in response. "Good thing you never

got to say it. I wouldn't have been able to stop myself from taking you right on the dance floor."

I squeezed and teased the swollen cockhead, which was nearly poking through the material, a wide circle of wetness there showing he was as eager as I was to get this party started.

I chuckled. "I wouldn't have stopped you."

I peeled his underwear off his body and, finally, we were standing naked in front of each other, the place we'd both wanted to be since the night we'd met. It felt almost too good to be true.

He eased me into his arms, kissed me, his lips sliding across mine, nipping, sucking, softly, relentlessly, completely. My knees quivered, and I was glad his arms were around me, mine around him, holding me up.

"Nick. Love me." Excitement turned my voice into a rough, needy whisper, but he heard.

He took my hands and climbed into bed, drawing me along with him, lying beside me. My breasts were heavy and ripe, my nipples puckered and begging for the touch of his hands and lips and tongue, and he gave them what they needed.

His hand cupped one breast, his thumb and finger pinching the puckered tip into a shape that fit his mouth perfectly. He leaned over to test it, running his tongue over it, flicking it, laving it, before taking it into his mouth.

I felt his cock jutting against my stomach, and I reached between us to grab it. Our bodies were so close I couldn't move much, but I held him, squeezed him, pinched the tip of him like his mouth was doing to my tips until he groaned and ground against me.

His mouth was back on mine, tasting me,

swallowing me, but inch by slow inch, his hands continued their trek downward, across my stomach. His fingers teased across my skin thoroughly before moving lower to tease and stroke the wetness between my thighs.

"Open your legs for me," he whispered against my mouth, his breath ragged. I eagerly parted them.

He greeted my pussy gently with his fingers, massaging my wet lips, rubbing them over my clit, eliciting a low moan of pleasure from me. I jerked a sharp breath into my lungs when his finger delved deep into my core and another continued the massage on my clit.

His cock was full and throbbing, grinding against me, desperate to bury itself deep inside my body. I wanted him inside me. My hand around his shaft moved with more purpose, wanting to encourage him to fill me now. But apparently he had plans I didn't know about, plans about heightening and extending our pleasure. He inched down my body until I could no longer touch him. He left kisses on my stomach, licks to my belly button, nips and sucks on my parted thighs, before settling his head between my legs.

The feel of him there, his breath against me, the sounds coming from him, launched me upward several notches on the pleasure scale, and my hands flew to his head to hold on. His lips tugged at my pussy lips like his fingers had, his tongue darted over the tiny bead, then drew a long slow line along my slick opening. Again and again. Making my hips rise to his mouth and crazy sex sounds grunt from my mouth at the pleasure of it all.

My release was imminent, dancing within my reach, but I didn't want to take it yet. I wanted to stay perched on the sharp edge, take more pleasure, give it. I wanted to ache in every cell of my body before letting go.

"Wait," I said in a hoarse whisper. He stopped, looked up at me, disappointment in his eyes for the interruption. I slid away from him and sat up, turned, aligning my mouth with his cock, his mouth to my pussy. He grinned, finally understanding.

"I want to taste you too," I said and grabbed his dick, licked him, sucked him, while he groaned his pleasure, stilling at the apex of a thrust as I took him in my mouth.

After a moment to gather himself, his arm hooked around my thigh and he held me open as his mouth went to my pussy, ate my flesh, and sucked my juice.

His hips pumped, drawing his cock in and out of my mouth, rough breaths leaving and entering his lungs. My hips pumped too, grinding my cunt into his face. He was close to coming. So was I.

"Now, baby. Fuck my cock," he groaned.

I rose and straddled him, his prick at my pussy, and he slid home, letting us feel every bit of each other. He pumped and I rocked. As if he could feel the urgency of my body, he rolled us over, so that he was on top. He increased the pace, sliding in and out, hard and fast, each stroke of his cock scraping my clit. His chest brushed across my nipples, making them ache.

His mouth swallowed my breath until I thought I'd lose my mind from the torrent of pleasure about to explode inside me. I couldn't hold on anymore.

My head flew back, a silent cry screaming my release, not even getting Nick's full name out, and I froze, clutching him, both from inside my body and out. He was right behind me, fighting to find his release in my willing, loving body. My pussy squeezed him, again and again, milked him, dragged him into pleasure with me, and he went eagerly, letting the powerful, shuddering explosion rock him as he arched his back up and slammed into me one last time.

"Every. Fucking time. With you is. So fu—fucking awesome," he said through ragged breath. His mouth was at my mouth, drawing in air, but mostly just my scent, my essence. I felt his body trembling on mine, as if the release had left him with no energy. "I love you more each time."

He kissed my mouth, claiming me. I kissed him back. Claiming him.

"I love you too," I whispered and encouraged him to sink into my body. Our hearts pounding on a single beat, we remained wrapped in and around each other, our lungs trying to catch a breath, our eyes trying to focus, our heads trying to think.

Soon, he rolled off me but kept me in his arms. Though our bodies were no longer connected, my body still hummed with satisfaction I'd never experienced with anyone but him. This moment rivaled that other moment, the night we'd first come together like this. In our perfect spot by the river.

He gazed into my love-hazed eyes. "Remember this moment, Angel," he said, running the tips of his fingers up and down my back slowly, and I cherished every goose bump his touch rose on my skin.

"I will. But why?" I asked.

"It's the first moment of the rest of our life together. You said you love me, I said I love you, and we just made love for the first time as a committed couple. Without a condom. We're a part of each other. No barriers. Physically or emotionally. No secrets."

His words touched me, so much so that I had to speak before I drowned in emotions. "I know you like it when I tell you you're right, but baby, you're only partly right."

He grinned. "Oh? Which part did I get wrong?"

"That moment happened a year, a month, and two weeks ago. The first time we were together like this."

He shook his head. "We didn't love each other then. We weren't even sure we would be with each other beyond that night."

"Yes, but it was a significant moment because it helped me see who I was and what I wanted and how to take the first steps to asking for it. Admit it—it was an important moment to you too."

"Yeah. I knew there was a solid chance I'd be getting regular sex from then on."

Laughing, I pinched his nipple. "Jerk!"

He laughed and grabbed my hand, kissing it. "Let me tell you how important it was. You and I had never spoken to each other before that night, but I knew who you were. Angela Nicole Abbott. The smartest, most beautiful, most desirable girl in school. The ice princess who demanded only the best of everything and accepted nothing less. And for some reason, you wanted me. Being with you that night made me feel like I mattered, like I was better than I really was, as good as I wanted to be. Hell, if you wanted me, I had to be fucking special, right? After that night, I wanted to be that person for you. I wanted to be someone you could love and be proud of."

"Baby, I wanted you from the first time I saw you," I said. "You rumbled up on your bike, black shades in place, looking like a badass. Your tight jeans hugged your ass and your legs, and I almost came just watching you strut across campus. I would sneak peeks at you whenever I could because I liked how it made my heart explode in my chest. I know it sounds like I was only hot for your bod, but it was more than that. There was something in you that called to me. Told me you were someone worth noticing. I've been writing about you in my journal since the first day I saw you."

"Why didn't you ever talk to me?"

"I didn't think you'd want to have anything to do with me. You avoided everyone like me. I was afraid you'd reject me, and I'd look like a fool. You, the badass, were always special to me. Always had a place in my heart. But the night we made love, I realized how really special you, Nick Spencer, were. For the first time in my life, I felt totally alive. I could breathe. I could taste. I could feel. *You* did that. That's how incredible you were. You mattered to me."

"I mattered to you. But you broke up with me."

"My mom warned me that you weren't the kind of guy a girl like me gets involved with, and that what happened between us had to be a one-time thing."

"You told her we had sex?"

"No. She knew. She said it was obvious by the way we looked at each other." The way we were looking at each other now, I imagined.

He nodded.

"On one of those days you gave me a ride home— the day your mom caught us in bed—my mom saw us kiss before you rode off, so she knew I hadn't given you up. I'd never seen her so furious. We were arguing, and she was saying horrible things about you—she'd read the report about you that Tyler's dad had contracted. I told her that you made me happy, and that I was with you whether she liked it or not. She said that if I didn't break it off with you, they could make things really difficult for you. I didn't know what she meant exactly, but I knew I didn't want them to hurt you."

"You broke up with me so they couldn't make trouble for me?"

"That was a big part of it, yes. But to be honest, it wasn't just them. It was me too. I loved you, and I wanted you, but I wasn't strong enough to go against everyone, to fight the fight to be with you. I had never felt like that before, and I was scared to trust you and our feelings. Instead of admitting what I wanted and fighting for it, I ran from it."

He was quiet for a moment. Maybe I'd been too honest.

"So what's changed?" he said finally, his voice flat. "Are you only with me now because no one here knows you? If we're for real, we'll have to fight the fight sooner or later with your family, your friends."

"Everything's changed. I don't care what anyone thinks about us. I only care about what you and I think about us. I trust you and our love. I know how horrible it feels to be without you, and I never want to feel that again. If you love me and want to be with me like I want to be with you, I won't give you up. Not for any reason. I'll fight to stay with you, Nick. I promise."

He looked at me like he wasn't sure he could believe me, then looked away. He still didn't trust me, didn't trust that I wouldn't leave him.

I sat up. "Hand me my purse." I pointed to it on the table beside us.

"Why?"

"Just do it."

He handed it to me, and I opened it, pulled out my

phone.

"What are you doing?" he asked.

I tapped in my passcode and scrolled through my contact list. "Calling my parents."

He sat up. "Why?"

"To tell them you and I are together."

"You do realize it's almost midnight."

"Yeah."

I put it on speakerphone and hit the HOME listing. It rang. Once. Twice. Three times. My dad's sleepy hello came through the speaker.

"Hi, Daddy. It's me."

"Angela? It's nearly midnight. Are you okay?"

Before I could answer, I heard my mom say, "Is she okay?" He answered, "She didn't say."

"Angela." Mom was on the phone now. "What's wrong?"

Nick mouthed the words, "I believe you. Hang up."

"Everything's great. I just called to say, I love you." Nick kissed my lips softly when I said I love you, staring right at him.

"Are you drunk?"

I laughed. "No, Mom. I'm not drunk. I'm…I'm happy. Hey, I might be coming home for a visit next weekend. I have some exciting news to share. That okay?"

"Of course, it's okay. You know we love seeing you. Tell me your news now."

"I need to go, but I'll talk to you soon."

"I'm glad you called. We miss you."

"Me too. Bye."

I hit END CALL. Nick lifted my phone from my hands and put it in my purse, setting it back on the table.

He held me to him as he lay back down. "I love you, and I'll fight to keep you too."

"You may have to," I said, playing with one of his nipples. "You do remember that I'm not your mom's favorite person, either. How do you think she'll react?"

"She won't like it any more than your parents will. But our relationship is *our* relationship. Not theirs. Whatever life throws at us, we'll get through it, as long as we stay strong, and stay together."

"You're right."

He grinned. "I love it when you say that." He rolled onto me, covering my body with his, and kissed me, showing me his love and his promises were as strong and forever as mine.

He *was* right—about everything. At that moment I knew, without a shadow of doubt, that Nick Spencer would never again be my dirty little secret.

Epilogue

Several years have passed since that night—we call it our night of awakening. Nick and I are still working at our relationship and our education. We live together in a little apartment off campus. We eat a lot of ramen noodles, eggs, beans, mac 'n' cheese, and canned tuna. Steak, our favorite food, is a rare luxury, and it doesn't come with a merlot sauce and English Stilton slivers.

We're poor, financially speaking, but that's only until we finish school. He's a semester away from finishing, and I'm not far behind. But we're rich in love, in happiness, in joy, and that's forever.

Nick and I did go see our parents the following weekend to tell them about us. Mine started in on what a mistake I was making, but I made it very clear I wouldn't listen to any negative comments about him or us. The argument escalated, and they threatened to withhold financial support for college unless I broke it off with him. I told them they had to do what they thought was right, just as I was doing.

They didn't cut me off, at least not then. But when I moved out of the dorm and into an apartment with Nick the summer before my sophomore year, they stopped paying my living expenses. Today, they still pay my tuition and a little each month for books, supplies, and food, but I'm responsible for everything else, like rent, utilities, gas, and any personal items.

I found a part-time job to make ends meet. When I turned twenty-one, I was able to dip into the inheritance my grandmother left me, but Nick hated when I did, saying that was for my future, not to whittle away at on everyday living.

To this day, my parents still can't understand my choice, and sadly it has affected our relationship. It doesn't seem to make a difference to them that I'm happy. Truly happy. To their minds, I chose wrong, and nothing I say or Nick does will ever change that. But who I love is my choice, not theirs. So, whatever. It's stupid of me, I know, but I keep hoping they'll come around eventually and see him through my eyes, see the wonderful man he is.

Nick's mom is a little less critical of our relationship—she at least visits us in our apartment now and then, usually with an armload of groceries or a casserole—but she still has it in her head that I'm holding him back, keeping him from reaching his full potential. She's worried I'll get pregnant and ruin his life. Mainly, she's terrified I'll leave him for another man, a man from my "world," that I'll break his heart like I did in high school. Maybe time will give her the proof she needs to realize that I won't do to him what her husband did to her. But even if it doesn't, that's no concern of ours.

We can't please our parents or anyone else, but it doesn't matter. Nick's the only one I care about pleasing, and he feels the same about me. Sure, like all lovers in an intense, passionate relationship, we have our challenges. Mainly it's stupid stuff, like whose turn it is to wash dishes or clean the bathroom, or who left the wet towel on the floor after his shower, or who left the TV on accidentally when she left for work. But like Nick and I agreed on the first day of the rest of our lives together, whatever life tosses our way, we'll deal with it, using the guiding principle that we'll do anything and everything to keep our love strong and our relationship intact.

The tie that binds us has been stretched thin, has even broken in places. But before it could twirl off in opposite directions, we grabbed both ends and tied them together to give us a sturdy holding place to grasp. The plan works because our never-changing truth is that the love we have for each other is real and precious and worth fighting for. Always.

About the Author

Welcome to love, picante style.

I began writing and selling short romances in college to support my bad habits then soon graduated to novel-length erotic romances, including *Dirty Little Secret* and *She Likes It Irish*.

I write the kind of books I like to read: stories where sexual heat sizzles off the page and the characters fall into lust and love. When I'm not writing about passion, I'm indulging in it—yoga, hiking, and laughing with friends over hot chile and cold beer.

Visit Sophia at
http://sophiaryan.webs.com

To chat with Sophia Ryan and other Wild Rose Press authors of erotic romance, join us at www.groups.yahoo.com/group/thewilderroses.

Also Available

She Likes It Irish

by

Sophia Ryan

http://amzn.com/B00BIW8Q3C

Kristin DeMarco vows to protect her broken heart and swear off men until she finishes her degree and starts her career. Survival sex—a vibrator and a sizzling-hot roommate—eases urges that can't be ignored, until her craving for a man propels her from the arms of Mr. Wrong to the door of Mr. Right. Irishman Sean O'Neill forces her to consider what she really wants. And what she wants is him in her bed. Too bad he's not cooperating.

Sean is only in America for six months to complete his degree and an archeology field school. He's as serious about his education as he is about keeping his sex life casual. When Kristin knocks on his door asking for condoms, the encounter forces him to rethink that single-minded focus. He wants Kristin for more than one night, but their secrets may end the relationship before it begins.

Chapter One

Randy fumbled with a key that seemed three sizes too big for the lock.

"Hurry!" Kristin's hungry whisper in his ear and a squeeze of the bulge in his jeans proved the magic combination to unlocking the door, and the two burst through into his dark dorm room.

Lips fought to stay connected as coats were yanked off. Boots kicked off. Shirts ripped away. Zippers scraped open. Jeans and underwear tangled hopelessly at ankles then wrestled off as one. Amid the clutching and grabbing, one of them remembered to kick the door closed before the soon-to-be lovers fell naked across the unmade, extra-long twin bed.

Kristin grabbed Randy's erection, stroking it. It wasn't as big as she'd hoped, but she moaned at the thought of it filling her slick, hungry tunnel, plunging in and out, stroking every nerve, like his probing fingers were trying to do.

The tension in her body ratcheted up, and her body ached for the hard, sweet KO that would give her what she needed so badly that she'd hook up with just about anybody. Even her somewhat socially awkward classmate.

Now, she screamed silently. *Oh, God, now!*

"Condom?" they asked in unison.

"What?" Again in unison.

"Fuck!" Three for three.

"You're kidding. What guy doesn't maintain a stock of condoms?" Kristin sat up and pushed out of the sexual fog that had made her somewhat desperate but, thankfully, not stupid.

Randy shrugged. "I, uh, ran out last weekend. C'mon, we could still have fun." He grinned and lifted his eyebrows. "We could do a sixty-nine."

She paused to consider the idea then quickly shook her head to dismiss it. She needed long, hard dick filling her, not a flicking tongue teasing her. In the moment of silence before her dream crashed and burned, the dull thump of a deep beat called to her through the wall from the room next door.

"What about your neighbor?" she asked, nodding her head toward the sound.

Randy's eyes rounded, and he looked a little scared. "You want him to join us?"

She released an exasperated sigh, complete with an eye roll. "No. Would he have condoms?"

"Uh, yeah, I'm positive he would, but it's not a good idea to ask him."

Kristin bounded out of bed at "yeah," grabbed one of the shirts piled on the floor, and pulled it on. From the cluttered desk, she grabbed a mug stuffed with pens and dumped them onto the floor with the rest of the mess.

"Kristin, wait," Randy began, but she ignored him and rushed out of the room, rapping on the neighbor's door.

The pounding beat blasted out of the room at Kristin when the door opened, a god standing at the door with a ridiculously large dumbbell in his hand.

The song commanded her to *look at that body*, and she did. Tall, ripped, glistening, and tight from his workout. Thick, blond, sun-kissed hair, a bit curly and endearingly unkempt, framed a made-in-heaven face. The man was as sexy as they come, from head to toe, made even more so by the fact that he wore nothing but boxers—green ones with red lips perched atop the words "Kiss The Legend" scrawled across the Blarney Stone.

A rush of lusty heat engulfed her body as his dark-as-dusk eyes gave her the same long, slow once-over before making their way back up to her face. Then his gaze tangled with hers, and she couldn't move. Breathed in but found no air in her lungs. Heart pounded so hard she was sure it would fly out of her chest. Goosebumps marched over her skin as his full lips curled into a wide, sexy smile. The floor moved under her feet, and she stuck out a hand and grabbed the doorjamb to steady herself.

"Well, hello, darlin'," he said in a thick Irish lilt that trilled across her skin like a caress and made her legs wobble. If his gaze hadn't been holding on so tightly to hers, she surely would have toppled over into his arms.

She couldn't stop the smile taking over her face. "It's Kristin." Her voice came out breathy and husky, and she felt her face warm at her intense and unexpected reaction to this stranger. But she kept her eyes on his as if her survival depended on it.

"What can I do for you…Kristin?"

The soft sound of her name on his lips made her go all gooey inside, struggling to remember why she had even come to his door in the first place. He moved a step closer, raised his arm, and leaned it on the doorjamb near her hand. The movement shifted his body closer to hers, and she could feel him, as if he was pressed against her. It suddenly became very clear why she was here.

Her eyes dipped down to the kiss on his boxers. Sex. Condoms. Her eyes rose to his again. He stared at her as if he was a heartbeat away from pulling her into his room and locking the door behind them.

She swallowed. When had her throat gotten so dry? Why was it so hot in here? Breathe, dammit!

"We're mixing something up next door," she finally said, nodding her head toward Randy's, "and wondered if we could borrow a cup of condoms." It had seemed like a good idea at the time, coming here to ask for condoms. Hearing the words come out of her mouth now, she knew it was a bad idea. Especially when a better idea had since formed, one that involved this Irishman pulling her into his room and using the condoms on her.

He blinked. "You want to borrow what?"

"A cup of condoms."

"Randy needs condoms?" He threw back his head and laughed. Before she could respond, Irish put the weight down and stepped out into the hall. He took her hand in his. "Darlin', let's you and I go have a little talk with your boyfriend."

"He's not my…" she started and then realized she should shut up.

Irish smiled and led her back to Randy's room, the empty cup dangling on one finger of her other hand.

Randy sat on his bed, dressed, his head slumped in his hands.

"Sorry, *boyo*. You want to tell the lass or should

I?" Irish said, the grin on his face suggesting he wasn't sorry at all.

"Tell the lass what?" Kristin asked, pretty sure she wasn't going to like the answer.

"You have to leave," Randy said, his voice thick.

She snorted with a laugh, but when no one else laughed, she lost her smile and stared at Randy. "You're kidding."

"No kidding," Irish responded when Randy couldn't seem to. "So, get your—"

She snatched her hand from his large, warm grip and stared into his sinful, devilish eyes. Her temporary interest in Randy was obviously a mistake, but she didn't like someone else making that decision for her. Especially the Irish hottie standing beside her, smiling like he was enjoying spoiling her plans, and enjoying her embarrassment. "Who are you? The sex police?"

He had the nerve to laugh.

"He's the RA. Sean," Randy explained, finally finding his voice. "He enforces dorm rules."

"What rules?"

"No women on the floor after midnight—it's now twelve forty-one—and I kick out the women I see," Sean answered.

The ones he SEES. His meaning dawned on her and she shook her head. "Ah. So, if I hadn't chosen *your* door to bang on—"

He nodded. "You'd still be holding an empty cup, but we wouldn't be having this conversation."

"This is ridiculous." She tossed the empty cup at Randy, who caught it and cradled it like something precious. She crossed her arms over her chest and glared at Sean. "We're grad students. Adults. We don't need anyone regulating our sex life." She turned her glare to Randy. He dropped his eyes to the floor—or to the cup again, she couldn't be sure. She shook her head in disgust.

"Get your clothes on, darlin'," Sean said, a chuckle in his voice that she found both endearing and annoying. "I'll escort you home."

"Thanks, but you've already been *too* helpful tonight." She hoped her sarcasm wasn't lost on him.

"Kristin…" Randy began.

She held up her hand to stop him. "Don't even."

Embarrassed to the tips of her toenails by this whole fiasco, Kristin rushed around the dimly lit room, tossing aside clothes, towels, books, and shoes to find her hastily discarded clothing, mumbling about little boys and their big egos, while the two guys watched quietly.

"How do you find anything in this dump? It's a health hazard. Why don't you enforce a rule about that, Mr. RA?" Spying her panties hanging on the lamp by the dresser, she quickly and discretely pulled them on, pretty sure she had flashed her pale cheeks to one or both of the guys, who were watching her intently when she turned around.

Sean held out a pair of skinny jeans that clearly didn't belong to Randy. "Yours?"

She grabbed them from his hand and, as she pulled them on, a flash of neon purple winked at her from a pile of clothes. She dug in and pulled out her shirt.

Turning her back to her audience, she stripped off Randy's shirt and tossed it onto the pile, wrinkling her nose at the unidentifiable smell clinging to it. As she was turning her own shirt right-side-out, she realized, too late, that she was standing in front of the full-length mirror hanging on the closet door.

Not only did she have a full view of Sean, but he had a full view of her.

His eyes held tight to her body, like a lion watches the gazelle he's stalking. The heat of his stare skated across her skin, and she felt the fine hairs on her body stand up. His eyes met hers in the mirror and he grinned, making her nipples pucker and her pussy tingle as if he'd touched them with that smiling mouth.

Her heart rose high in her throat and she tried to swallow, but her mouth was too dry. *Oh, shit!* She remembered that feeling swirling through her heated flesh like liquid heat. It wasn't simple attraction. It was lust. Desire. Pure. Red-hot. Hungry.

What was wrong with her? How could she crave this perfect, hot, gorgeous, sexy-as-hell man she knew nothing about other than his name?

This was not good.

After almost two years of staying away from men, two in one night had seen her bare breasts and her naked ass. One of them she never wanted to see again. The other she wanted to donate her body to.

Pulling her shirt on forced her eyes away from his, but did nothing to staunch the loud humming in her body that said, "Gotta have me some of that."

Careful to keep her eyes from the mirror, she found her jacket near the door and put it on, zipping it to her chin. One boot stood against the desk, along with her backpack.

"I can't find my bra," she said as she stuffed one foot into the boot. "It's pink, it's expensive, and it makes my breasts look spectacular, so I want it back."

When she straightened, Sean stood at her side, the matching boot in his hand. She tried to avoid his eyes, but they compelled her to look. So she did. They looked into her, holding her, devouring her. He wanted her, too!

A sigh purred up from her throat, but she swallowed it before it could leave her mouth. Taking the boot from his hand, she dropped her eyes to focus on pulling it on, then rushed to the door. She picked up her backpack and slung it over her shoulder as she looked back at Randy.

"You do your half of the project, I'll do mine, and *this*," she wagged her finger between the two of them, "never happened."

"Kristin…" Sean and Randy both began as she flung open the door.

"Give me a sec to get dressed," Sean said.

"Sorry," Randy whined.

She ignored them both and rushed out of the room, leaving the door open. She was down the stairs, out the front door, and several yards away from that dorm of regret when she heard footsteps clomping behind her on the crusty, frozen ground. Had Randy decided to do the right thing and walk her home? A glance over her shoulder told her it wasn't Randy, but Sean jogging toward her. He had pulled on a thick hooded sweatshirt and hiking boots, which he'd left untied, but only those thin boxers covered his lower half.

Frigid air assaulted her lungs and nose when she breathed in, and she was cold even wearing jeans, boots, and a jacket. Guilt rose in her like foggy breath, knowing that Sean's bare legs were probably freezing in the thirty-two-degree February night.

"I'm fine on my own, really," she said. "Go back in before you freeze."

"Which dorm are you in?" He pulled the hood over his head and tucked his hands in the pockets at the stomach, ignoring her insistence that she was fine.

Fine, let him freeze. "Zia."

"On the other side of campus?"

His shivering legs and chattering teeth brought a little smile to her face. "That's the one. Still think I need an escort?"

"I kicked you out, so it's my job to protect you. If your cute little arse got assaulted walking across campus at one in the morning, I couldn't live with myself."

She stared into desire-filled eyes, remembering his sinfully hot body, and, God help her, what was inside those damn-ugly boxers. "Who's going to protect me from you?"

He laughed.

She didn't. "You do realize frostbite hits large exposed areas first?"

"Aye. I also realize those areas are less likely to freeze if I keep moving, so if you don't mind…"

They trudged across the still campus, the only sounds their footsteps on the icy brown grass, their breathing, and the occasional chattering of Sean's perfect white teeth.

"Most of the guys on the floor have come to my door for condoms. But tonight's the first time a beautiful, half-naked woman has asked for a whole cup."

"Hmm, well, don't be impressed or anything. It was just plain old desperation that sent me to your door," she said, thankful for the darkness that hid her smile. He had called her beautiful.

"Desperation? For condoms or because you regretted your choice of partners?"

"Wow," she said with a scoffing chuckle. "Someone has a high opinion of himself."

"You didn't answer my question."

"Look," she said, and stopped, turning to face him. "It's been a really long time since I…"

She couldn't concentrate with his dark eyes shining, smiling, staring deeply into hers as if he were absorbing her every word and very interested in learning how long she had been celibate.

Swirling sensations of awareness for this perfect stranger were stirring up long-buried wants and needs. The heat of his body rushed out to meet hers, and, oh God, she could smell him, a delicious aroma of soap and sweat and man that made her want to lick him all over. She wanted to ask him to plant his flag in her and claim her for his own. Right here. Right now.

His very presence, his nearness, sucked the air from her lungs. And he grinned at her like he could read every single thought slip-sliding through her passion-filled brain. She strong-armed her inner slut back and tore her eyes from his, but that didn't make the sensations burst like soap bubbles as she'd hoped.

"Never mind." She started walking again, then stopped when she noticed he wasn't beside her. She looked back. In the light of the half moon, she thought she saw his eyes glued to her butt. She spun around to face him.

"Are you looking at my ass?"

The grin he gave her said, "Aye, I was." But his mouth said, "Why don't you have a boyfriend taking care of your needs?"

"That's none of your business." She turned her back to him and continued walking, smiling when he jogged to catch up.

"Girls like you usually have loads of boyfriends to pick from."

She stopped again, facing him with a spark of anger. "Girls like me? What's that supposed to mean?"

"Ones with gorgeous green eyes that could stop a man's heart and sweet lips that could bring him back to life with a single kiss."

Though she knew a line of bull when she heard it, that damn sexy accent sent chills skating up and down her body and left her blushing and struggling for a response that didn't include giggling or babbling.

"I'm not *incapable* of getting a boyfriend, if that's what you're suggesting."

"I didn't say that."

"I'd have one if I wanted one."

His eyes were staring so deeply into hers that she was sure he could read the real reason she didn't have a boyfriend. She lost her mind completely when he reached out and brushed a thick strand of hair from her face with his fingertips. Her skin heated under his touch and her bones began to slowly melt.

"Do you?" Sean breathed the words more than spoke them.

Shit! She'd forgotten the question. "Do I what?"

"Want someone?"

"What I want is…" *Oh, my God, you!* "…to focus on finishing my degree."

"Can't you juggle the books and a lover at the same time?"

"I could. I choose not to." She kept walking and

took a deep breath to steady herself. He was right beside her.

After a short pause, he interrupted the quiet night again with another question. "Would you like to know whether I have a girlfriend?"

Oh, God, yes! "I have a feeling you're going to tell me whether I want to know or not."

"I'm unattached...like you."

"What!" she said, increasing the volume of her sarcasm. "You mean a charming guy such as yourself hasn't found someone special even with a whole campus full of women to choose from? Hot-blooded American women, by the way, who fantasize about dropping their drawers for a guy with an Irish brogue."

"Tell me, Kristin, is this your fantasy as well?" She felt his hand brush hers, and then one finger hooked hers, sending tingles up her arm and straight to her heart. "If so, I'd be happy to make it come true."

Her face burned hot in the cold night as her mind scanned her list of top ten fantasies and found being with an Irish hunk sitting at *numero uno*. It was crazy how he knew just what to say to stop her heart. It was as if he could see inside her, see all her bottled-up secrets that longed to come out and be shared with that special someone she'd been looking for her entire life. *Damn him!*

She struggled for control over her emotions and moved her hand away from his. "Now I understand the problem. With that ego, I bet you're looking for someone with the face of a movie star, the body of a model, the skills of a porn star, and the IQ of a gnat."

He stopped and grabbed her hand so she would stop, too. His gaze locked on hers as he slid his hand around her waist and settled it at her lower back. Applying almost imperceptible pressure, he maneuvered her closer until mere inches separated her body from his.

"No," he said, his voice somewhere between a whisper and a caress. "I'm looking for a woman who is so filled with passion that she'll beat down a stranger's door for a cup of condoms just to have me."

Cold air wrapped around them in the stillness, uniting them. Breaths of steam exited their mouths in sync, mated in the air, and dissipated as one.

Shivering to dislodge the troupe of chill bumps that had settled down on her like snowflakes, she swallowed and steadied herself to speak.

"Don't mistake my actions," she answered, her voice low and soft, like she was confessing her sins to him. "I just needed someone tonight."

"I don't mistake your passion." His voice matched hers in tone and volume, once again showing how in sync they were. "I saw it on your face when I opened my door." He ran his thumb along her jaw line then touched the corner of her mouth. "And it wasn't for Randy."

He was right, of course. The second he'd opened his door, she had known without a single doubt that Randy had been a mistake. The desire she had felt for Sean at that moment was still alive and well. She could feel it, and he could see it. His eyes roamed hungrily over her face. She felt the warmth of his touch and his breath on her skin. Smelled his hard body, his desire. She felt the tug of him deep inside her. He wanted her, she wanted him. All the pieces were in place.

It would be a simple thing to shift closer, ease

deeper into his embrace. Lift her mouth to his and let his kisses drive away all thoughts from her troubled mind. Let his hands remind her that she was a woman, with a woman's need for a man. And not just any man...a man like him. No, not *like* him...*him*. Let his sexy, hard body satisfy that need. And he could do it. Of that she was fully convinced. The man radiated strength and sexual prowess. He would know how to fuck a woman, how to please her, to distraction.

Even as she shivered at the idea of what he could do to her, she knew it would be a mistake. He was her type—a love-her-and-leave-her kind of guy who would thrash her heart as easily as he had won it—unfortunately. The type she was trying to stay away from. She forced herself to step back from his embrace.

"Why would you think that?" she said and turned away from him to keep walking.

"Because Randy's not your type," Sean said, right by her side.

Shit! Was he a mind reader, too? "After knowing me for all of, what, five minutes, you're an authority on my type?"

"I know the guys on my floor. Randy's definitely wrong for you."

"I hope the university is paying you mega bucks for your amazing talents of deduction."

"No mega bucks. But I do get to escort beautiful women to their dorm."

She felt her heart swell as his meaning sank in. That was twice he'd called her beautiful. "Doesn't sound like much of a reward, if you ask me," she said.

"All of life's miracles are rewarding, darlin'. Some are just more...pleasurable." At the last word, he let his eyes roam over her body, then took a deep breath and released it slowly.

His emphasis on the word, and the knowledge that he appreciated her body, settled hot and heavy between her legs. Realizing she was holding her breath, she exhaled.

"Is that some old Irish saying?"

"New Irish saying. I made it up myself. Just now. Are you impressed?"

"I'm impressed you can still move after being out in this cold without pants."

"If you're worried about me, you could invite me in." He nodded his head toward the building looming before them. "A little body-to-body contact could save my life."

Sudden and deep regret filled her when she saw they were already at the entrance to her dorm. "Well, I would, but men aren't allowed in the dorms after midnight. And it's now," she glanced at her wrist where her watch would be if she'd worn it, "later than that. But thanks for the escort."

She turned away from him and grabbed the door. It wouldn't budge. Locked.

"Shit." She cupped her hands on the window and peered into the building to check for any movement. The front desk and reception area, which closed at one, were dark and deserted.

"Lost your key in that mess at Randy's?" he asked.

"No. It's in my room, sitting on my desk." She tapped her head on the window, feeling like an idiot.

"Can you call someone to let you in?"

"My phone's sitting next to my key, so I don't have anyone's number."

"Now that's a real shame. Well, good night." He held up his hand and turned to leave.

Regret scurried across her skin. "You're just going to leave me here? Alone? In the dark?"

He turned back to her, and the warm gleam in his eyes chased away the chill sheeting her skin.

"I'll stay... If you warm me up." He stepped closer as if to pull her against him, but she moved back and crashed into the glass door.

"It's your fault we're out here, Irish. If you'd just stayed out of my business, we'd both be warm right now."

"You invited me into your business when you knocked on my door, asking for condoms. Who's your RA?" he said, pulling his phone from his pocket.

She shrugged. "I don't know. Natalia something."

"Nattie Jones?"

"Yeah, maybe."

He punched in several numbers. "You'd have been warm but miserable because you slept with the wrong guy. Hey, Nattie. Sean O'Neill. Good. You? Oh, sorry to wake you, but I'm downstairs with one of your residents who needs in. Fantastic. Thanks, love." He hung up. "She'll be right down."

"My, aren't you the charmer. I could hear her giggling from here."

"Now, darlin', don't be jealous and hating on poor Nattie."

"Jealous?" she scoffed. "Why would I be jealous?"

"I saw you checking out my boxers."

Heat bloomed in her cheeks as Kristin fought to keep her mind and her eyes off his boxers—well, what was in his boxers. She couldn't help herself. Her gaze went right to where the red lips seemed to pout atop the Blarney Stone. The material rose. She shifted her eyes quickly to his face. To the sexy little grin on his face. To his laughing eyes. *Busted!*

The buzzer sounded and the door clicked, signaling that it was unlocked and she could turn away from those smug, knowing eyes.

"Good night, Blarney Stone," she said and reached for the handle, but he was already behind her, opening the door for her.

"Sleep well, darlin'." The whisper in his voice tickled her ear, and she turned to face him. He was so close she could smell the minty sweetness of his breath. So close she could see that his eyes were indigo not black. So close that if she lifted her face but a few inches she could taste his lips.

Sean was absolutely right: Randy was the wrong guy for her in every way. Sean, on the other hand, was looking more and more like a wish she had made on a four-leaf clover. Despite the fact that his body shivered from the cold, he was holding the door for her until she got inside. He didn't know her, but had escorted her all the way home in the cold February weather and stayed until she was safely inside her building. Randy hadn't even offered and she knew him—had been heartbeats away from sleeping with him.

The tenderness she felt for Sean at that moment lifted her hand to his shoulder. She let her hand slide down his arm slowly from shoulder to wrist, her fingers caressing every muscle along the way and helping her remember what they looked like without the jacket covering them. "Thank you."

He caught her hand when it ended its trek and slid

his fingers softly between hers, casually linking them. "For walking you home or for ruining your night?"

"Both," she said. "And sorry if anything…" she glanced down, "…froze."

"If it did, it was worth it."

She smiled. "Well…see you around."

"Count on it." He winked at her.

She turned to go in, and he let her hand slip away.

"Oh, about your breasts…" he started.

She nearly ran into the door spinning back toward him. "What?"

"Never mind. You better get inside. G'night." He smiled, released the door, and moved away slowly, still facing her.

"No, tell me," she said.

Sean was just out of reach. She could grab his arm, stop him, get him to finish his comment, but she'd have to let go of the door. A girl doesn't let a comment about her breasts go she reasoned as the door locked in place behind her.

"Sean," she said, grabbing his arm.

"Yes?" he teased, the ever-present smile in place.

"Tell me!"

He reached his hand into his sweatshirt pocket, pulled out something pink, and held it up by a strap. Chuckling, she lifted her bra from his finger, but he closed his finger over the strap before she could free it.

"Just so you know—it's not this pink thing that makes your breasts look spectacular."

Her breath left her lungs, and she longed to yank him hard against her and kiss the breath from his lungs.

"Are you coming in or not?" someone shouted from the door.

The voice broke their connection and they turned toward it. Nattie stood in the open doorway, hands on her round hips, blonde hair wound up in a massive clip.

Sean released Kristin's bra and she stuffed it inside her jacket.

"I'm giving up my beauty sleep holding the door open for you," Nattie said. "Not to mention freezing my ass off."

"Nattie, love," Sean said. "If you get any more beauty sleep, you'll have to keep the men away with a Taser."

She giggled. "Sean, you do my ego good. Now kiss her goodnight so I can get back to my warm bed."

Sean looked at Kristin and grinned. "You heard her, darlin'," he said and stepped closer. "She thinks I should…" his hands settled low and hot on her hips and he eased himself against her, "…kiss you."

The touch of his fingertips, his palms, burned through her jeans and singed her skin all the way to her toes. Hot and achy tendrils tugged at her core as he moved even closer, the Blarney Stone brushing against her, his breath warming her lips. He was going to kiss her, and she was going to let him. There were a lot of reasons to stop him. But as her brain fogged over with desire, she couldn't think of one.

Unfortunately, she didn't have to stop him. He stopped on his own. And she realized with a cold and hurtful shock that she was deeply disappointed. Time stood still as he stared into her eyes, and she waited for him to say why.

"When I kiss you for the first time, I want you to taste only me in your mouth." He backed away slowly then, maintaining eye contact. A few paces away, he turned and ran back across campus. Pretty fast for someone wearing half-laced boots and thin boxers, she noted before she went in, floating on a warm, fluffy cloud.

Also Read

Johnny Loves Krissy

by

KyAnn Waters

http://amzn.com/B003L77O6W

Kristina Taylor's biological clock just went off. She has endometriosis. Now "who's your baby's daddy" just took on a completely new meaning. A brilliant plan for conception includes her hot best friend Johnny Huston. Taking him to bed won't be a hardship—if she can only get him to play by her rules. After all, she wants to maintain their friendship. Not easy if he ends up being the best sex of her life.

Knock her up? Krissy has to be crazy. Or is she? Johnny has loved her since high school. Her plan might not include life after baby. His does. But how will he show her how good they can be together with all her rules—no kissing, no touching, no caressing? He can make love to her, but she's determined not to enjoy it. To hell with that and to hell with her rules. He's determined to show her friendship is the best foundation for a relationship.

But there are always complications…

With Johnny, Krissy is afraid to look to the future. Right now, she can't get enough of the present, and she dreads the thought of losing what she's had with him in the past.

www.ingramcontent.com/pod-product-compliance
Lightning Source LLC
Chambersburg PA
CBHW070048260626
47160CB00004B/1136